Love or Loyalty

Love or Loyalty

Part 1: The Beginning

Shateria A Franklin

PROLOUGE

So like any other book you read you picked it up looked at the cover and read the back you probably thought to yourself typical ghetto love story, well you're completely wrong this shit is far from typical. Oh yeah, I'm Lauren by the way, Lauren Young to be politically correct. I am 27 years old and I been through a hell of a lot. I guess some of it was necessary learning experiences but the rest was just the bullshit that came with the hand I was dealt. If you ask people about me some would just say I was a privileged little bitch that had everything handed to me. That is half-true but you know what they say believe only half of what you hear. But don't worry I'll break this shit all the way down so you understand just exactly who the fuck I am and you can form your own opinion.

I'm quite established at this point in my life but like I stated it wasn't always this way. I have been in and out of love, with and without money. I have experienced some of the most traumatic things but I survived it all because I was a natural born survivor. I had to be on top and for that reason alone I NEVER stopped. Oh and let us make this clear the difference between me and a lot of bitches is that I work hard for my spot at the top. I didn't fuck the boss or tear anyone down to get here I got it on my own from hard work and dedication. So yes, I feel entitled to the life I live and I deserve the man that God sent my way. Oh and I am not judging anyone just getting everything established before I let you in my life.

CHAPTER 1 - 1989

Lauren:

"Daddy" I yelled up the stairs loudly on this particular Saturday. Unlike most, I had my daddy growing up so that made me far from the average "looking for love in all the wrong places" type of chick. I had both my parents as a matter of fact, don't get me wrong we were not the Huxtables but my parents been married for 20 years and they provided a pretty decent life for me and my three siblings. I am the youngest and the most spoiled, you know your usual daddy's girl but times 10. I believed any man I had should be exactly like my father. Daddy was a hustler and a provider and he loves the shit out of us. My mom and dad had that high school sweetheart love and had no others outside their marriage. You would think with that kind of example I would have followed the same. Once again wrong, I sure knew how to pick all the wrong kind of niggas.

I heard him coming down the stairs "what's up baby girl" daddy kissed me on the forehead just like he did any other day.

"Oh nothing just gonna go to the mall with London, can I have some money pleaseee?"

"Don't tell your sister" daddy said with a smile and a wink. I was his soft spot and could get whatever at any time and he would not even blink an eye. I knew they were all jealous shit I think it even got under my mom's skin how my dad treated me like a little princess. But shit at 17 years old I wasn't doing too much. All my friends were on their second child and doing all kinds of slow shit. I was three months from graduating high school and 6 month from attending NYU on a full scholarship. Yes I was fucking but I wasn't about to let no one fuck up my chance at getting away from this town and making a name for myself. I wanted to be a brand. I wanted to be my own BOSS and that is exactly what I would do in the Big Apple. At least that is what I thought but God had other plans and I was forced to take the extremely long way to get to my goal.

London and I headed to the mall and with her that always meant trouble. She had a different kind of money, it wasn't because of daddy either this bitch was a certified gold digger and only fucked with ballers and I mean REAL ballers she was also a real estate agent. But she wasn't a hoe I didn't get it she could get whatever from any man and she wasn't giving them too much in return. My big sister was todays definition of a "BAD BITCH" she had these niggas on smash and I looked up to her she was extremely gorgeous just like a China Doll. I mean we were all easy on the eyes we got it from our momma, which happened to be the baddest 46 year old walking around Charlotte, everyone loved Mama Jackie she had a stupid dumb booty and this small waist. I see why my dad loved her she was the shit and she definitely passed on her looks to her daughters. Even my two brothers were "fine as hell" as all my friends would say. I would be rich if I had a dollar for every time one of them hit on my dad or brothers. Jamie was 28 and Kyree was 32 they were also everything that I would not date. They had these hoes going crazy. I just laughed because they stayed in my business but had enough drama for the whole family. "Bitch do you hear me" London said snapping me out of daydream she continued to talk about this bag she knew I would love and would buy as an early graduation present. "You know we are all proud of you especially daddy" London smiled

"You were serious about leaving us and going to the Big Apple, I bet it's some fine ass ballers up there" she said. "Bitch, that all you think about" I said laughing as we headed into the mall.

I must admit these would be the moments I would miss being away from home just hanging with my sister now I was going to a new city with some new bitches that probably wouldn't like me because I'm cute.

It was not until we were about 3 hours in that I noticed I had left my phone in the car and London's phone had died. We knew we had to get the heck out this mall. When we got to the car I had 7 missed calls from mom, 5 from Jamie and 6 from Kyree something was up. Shit I did not know who to get back to first so I called mom and I instantly knew something was wrong when my grandma Mimi answered the phone. "Hurry to the house now" she said in a low voice. We pulled into the driveway and

noticed everyone's car there and it was safe to say
something bad had happened. We walked in the house
and all eyes instantly fell upon me. My mom was in the
kitchen taking to Mimi balling. What stood out to me the
most was that daddy wasn't in the midst of all the people.

"What's going on?" was all I could manage to say. But
my ears would have never been ready for the words that
uttered out my Kyree's mouth.

"Dad is dead," he said.

Everything went blank, I could see their lips moving but I
couldn't hear the words, my knees became weak and my
chest seemed so tight. Kyree reached out and caught me
just as my numb body began to fall to the ground.

"Where is my daddy?" I screamed over and over and
over. I sobbed so loudly into my brother's chest. The look
that was on my mother's face had confirmed that this was
not a test and this was the real fucking deal. But why the

fuck would God take my dad, what have I ever done to him for him to take the only person in the world whose soul matched mines. None of this made any sense my dad was the strongest, smartest man alive. He was careful, calculated and cautious at all times with everything and everybody.

"Lauren" I heard my mom call me from in the kitchen her voice was so weak. She held out her arms and hugged me so tight. She kissed my forehead and told me everything would be okay that she had me.

"Your dad had a massive heart attack on his way into the club and by the time one of the girls got there he was already nonresponsive" she said. I held up my hand for her to stop as she was about to tell me more. I didn't care for the details none of that fucking mattered. None of that bullshit would bring my daddy back and all I had left were precious memories.

In the matter of minutes, my life had changed forever.

Jayson

"It's always about the money fam" Jayson yelled into the phone hanging it up instantly. These niggas don't never do shit correct if you want something done you gotta do it yourself damn. The glitz of this life is the easy part but most niggas don't wanna do the work and that's the only way to make your mark in this game. I never wanted this life I guess it was just my fate. I was around this shit literally all my life, all I knew growing up drugs and money. I jumped in this game head first as a young nigga and I been getting money ever since. Life gave me lemons and I turned the shit into lemonade but it wasn't always good times. I had a hard ass life I had to learn everything from experiences most of them bad but I was so used to the shit that I didn't know what the fuck good really was. Only thing good in my life was my grandma and even she wasn't around to see me become a man. I can't help but wonder if just maybe she hadn't died if I would've turned out to be something else. I can picture her face and the things she would say.

I did have my mom and shit but she wasn't your average loving mother. She was unique in her own way and I didn't agree with her way of doing shit so we don't see eye to eye. As for my dad fuck that nigga he don't really deserve my thoughts because he aint teach me shit in life about being a man and everything I did see when he was around was some bullshit that no kids should see. There's no way this niggas should ever call himself a dad we aint have no father and son talks and I didn't go to that nigaa if I needed advice. All I had was mistakes, mistakes and more mistakes until I got it somewhat right. One thing I did learn from my parents is to be nothing like they ass when I have my own kids.

It all started when I discovered that you didn't have to go to work every day to get money and most of the dope boys on the block had much more than the average working muthafucka anyways. I remember asking for a pair of Jordan's and my momma told me she wasn't spending that much money on no damn sneakers. That was enough for me to realize I had to get some money of my own to get the things I wanted. I was not about to be no bummy ass kid getting picked on. So I turned to the block and at 12 years old I started getting money and from that day forward cocaine was my best friend. I was young as fuck getting to the money but what separated me from the other niggas was my hustle drive. I had more drive then some niggas double my age, I was hungry and I wanted to provide for myself but I also was young and I wanted to impress the bitches. I wanted all the bitches and the fly shit fuck that I wanted to be that nigga. I achieved just that I was that nigga but being that nigga comes with a hefty price. Especially where I come from nobody wants to see anyone doing better than them. See most muthafuckas only wanna tell the ups of the game but fail to mention that it's more downs then ups but I'm gonna keep it real with ya'll no sugar coating shit.

Lauren

It was summer 2010 when I let my crazy cousin Shay talk me into moving with her to this small ass town in Pennsylvania called Erie. I didn't even know where it was on the map but I was freshly graduated from Brooklyn Law School and she was a paralegal at a firm that was looking for a young new attorney so why not cause life in the NYC was expensive and it was hard to find any law firms to work for. I mean growing up in the Queen City it was a huge change and I mean huge but, I caught on quick that the bitches here are all in competition and the niggas well that's another story. It was so small that everyone knew everyone. There were no highways and tons of buildings like I had been used to. They were definitely not up to speed like this city girl and being the new bitch in town was hard at first cause it seemed everyone wanted to know who the fuck I was wherever I went. I thought I was gonna have to check a few bitches about they broke ass niggas tryna push up on me but thank God it never came to that.

This particular summer night Shay took me out to some club downtown, now there downtown was much different then back home but the club was really nice and it was jammed packed. I was looking good as hell in my all white Alexander McQeeen tight fitted dress with white and gold Tom Ford heels. My natural looking makeup was flawless because I never wore a lot just a tough to finish off my look. My long hair swung down just at the top of my round ass. Which I must add is all mines in an era of "inches" I take pride in my long real hair. I was killing shit with a capitol K. Shay and I made our way through the crowd she stopped introducing me to almost everyone we past. Shay was that bitch cause she had it going on here she was a boss and she worked hard in life which was why she was my favorite cousin we were cut from the same cloth always chasing a check. It seemed like all eyes were on me as I made my way to bar to get us a round of drinks. "Get me a henny with coke on the side" I heard Shay say over the music. I scanned the room briefly just to check my surrounding my city instincts always made me do so and in the VIP section I noticed a group of people that seemed to be celebrating. For a brief moment I locked eyes with one of the guys but quickly turned making my way to the main bar. As I was ordering our drinks the beautiful young bartender told me that all my drinks for the night had been paid for. I chuckled to myself wondering which one of these niggas could've pulled that off. But I was used to that and my daddy always reminded me not to let any man think he could impress me by buying a drink. Respectfully declining the offer I reached into my Chanel clutch and started a tab. I spotted Shay on the dance floor and joined her; the DJ was jamming all night. He played all the new shit mixed with some old too he had the whole club up and jumping.

We headed to our section in the VIP and danced the night away our server kept the drinks flowing and we turned the hell up it was a great night. The vibe and atmosphere in the club was nice it was a very good time shit we didn't leave the club until 4am and then headed to breakfast. Shay invited a few of her friends that were pretty cool chicks and we ate and laughed until about 6am. My old ass ain't been out till the sun came up since my freshman year in undergrad. We finally headed home and I had to tell Shay about what happened at the bar.

"Oh let me tell you when I went to the bar to get our drinks the first time someone had paid for our drinks for the night?"

"Bitch what? Who?" she said

"Girl I don't know shit I turned it down"

"Are you serious with your boujee ass? Girl that had to been one of them balling ass niggas it's only a few in the whole damn city"

"Well bitch I don't know and I don't care whoever the niggas is can keep his money cause you know this pussy cannot be bought" I said

"Shit they can buy mines" said Shay

"Shaking my damn head bitch you don't got no sense and
I know you serious I'm gonna put a for sale sign on your
ass" I laughed.

We laughed and finally we were home. I took a shower
and got straight in the bed my ass was tired. Although the
thoughts of who the mystery person was consumed my
mind I brushed it off and went to sleep.

I was getting settled into Erie life quite well. It
had been a few weeks, I already found a house, and I
would be starting my new job next week. Things were
definitely looking up since I had left all the madness in
North Carolina and NYC.

"I might as well start unpacking" I thought aloud looking
around at all the boxes wishing daddy was here to help
me. I still never got used to doing things on my own even
after all these years of his death.

There was a knock at the door, which was strange because I knew Shay was at work. I looked and it was a delivery truck, thinking nothing of it since I had been ordering so much shit for my house online. I opened up the door and sitting there was about 3 dozen red roses.

"Awe one my brothers sent me some flowers" I said

I noticed the card read, "You're hard to get with"

Now I was puzzled I just talked to Jamie yesterday and Kyree texted me this morning. Therefore, these flowers were definitely not from them. I do not know anyone here but Shay and her few friends who were girls so who the hell is sending my ass flowers.

I peeked my head out the door and nothing looked suspicious but then again I don't know what the hell the norm is around here I just moved in.

Oh well, they are pretty I thought so I placed them on my mantle and kept on unpacking. I had not stopped until my house was fully put together and by that time it was 9:00pm. Everything looked like I had been living there for a long time. It wasn't empty like when you first move into a new place. I knew Shay ass would be off work soon and heading over to any minute and since I hadn't eaten all day I decided to whip us up something to eat. I knew giving her a key probably was not a good idea. This bitch came busting through the door like it was her house talking all loud on the damn phone. "Fuck them bitches anyway they aint nothing but hood rats just mad." Shay laughed into the phone.

"Alright girl we will be there and I'm sure Lauren will be down she aint got shit to do anyways." Hanging up the phone and heading into the kitchen where I was finishing the food. If looks could kill she would fall dead right where she stood talking all loud in my damn house. Then telling people I aint got shit to do how she know I don't have a damn date. She better be glad she was my favorite cousin.

"Hey boo" she said smiling

"Hey bitch witcho loud ass mouth, oh and what will Lauren be down with?" I asked

"Girl that was Benita there is a party up in Farrell tonight some heavy hitter birthday party. I told her we would come" she said.

"No baby, I am dead tired I just put this whole house together all by my damn self this bitch is going to bed" I said

"You're such an old fucking lady, be ready by 11:30 – 12 cause we going it's Friday night it's nothing else to do. You'll be starting work next week so we gotta get it in while we can miss big time attorney. Oh and let's take your car."

"Bitch you a trip you know that? So your force me to go out and you wanna burn my damn gas?" I said.

"I'm going to get dressed and I'll take my plate to go I can eat while I'm getting dressed cause that shit smell soooo good." She grabbed her plate and was out the door just as quick as she came in.

Since I obviously didn't have a choice I got dressed for this party not really feeling like it but whenever I stepped out I had to be flawless. I applied just a touch of makeup like always to set off my lashes and perfect eyebrows. I slipped on a tight black leather dress that zipped up the front. Simple but hugged my body in all the right places, then I placed my freshly manicured toes into my all black so Kate Louboutin's. My hair was swept into a high messy bun that set my look over the top. A bitch was looking good very effortlessly I must say. If nothing went right tonight at least I could take a cute ass picture.

Shay pulled up at 11:30 on the dot looking equally fabulous in her tan mini skirt with matching crop top. Her gold Giuseppe heels made her tower over me by a few feet. Normally I don't let anyone drive my car but I didn't know where I was going anyways so I let Shay drive and I damn sure would be passenger seat driving. People always wonder why I am so funny acting about my car and trust me it had nothing to do with the fact that it was an all-black Range Rover with all black 22's and tinted windows. It was simply because daddy bought this car for me way before I could even drive all because it was my dream car. I remember just sitting inside of it in the garage waiting until the day I got my license and could drive. It was probably my most precious gift that reminded me of the only man that still owned my heart.

Shay's reckless driving snapped me out of my daydream.

"Bitch you better drive my shit better than that" I said with attitude.

"Oh my bad I am not tryna get murdered about your baby" said Shay

"You're absolutely right hoe" I laughed to loosen the mood but she knew I was serious.

We made it to the parking lot of the party and as usual all eyes scanned my car as we pulled up most certainly not something people was used to a young black female driving. Shay pulled up to the valet and we hoped out like celebrities walking through the entrance of the club with ease. Damn they act like they never seen pretty bitches before. These niggas were nothing like the ones in Erie they were much flashier and way more aggressive.

Like normal we headed to our section in the VIP right next to us in the section over was a group of guys and they were fine and checking for us. Immediately one stepped over and began talking to Shay. Most men always stepped to Shay first because her look was always more inviting than mines sometimes I could come off as boujee or not wanting to be bothered and normally that was accurate. I continued to sip my drink and enjoy the vibe unbothered. I felt a pair of eyes on the side of my face so I turned that was when we made eye contact, smiled, and looked away.

There was something different about him of all the guys surrounding him he was much more laid back. His demeanor screamed BOSS!! He was very well dressed in what looked like some foreigner designer. He was extremely handsome and obviously engaged in something important because other than our brief eye contact he kept his head in his phone.

Suddenly the server came over with 2 bottles of Ace of Spade Champagne and said it was on the house.

There was a note on the tray that said "you're still very hard to get with" that was the same damn thing that those flowers said. I noticed the guy from the section making his way over to us. Before I could say anything, he extended his hand to shake mines.

"My name is Jayson and you are?"

There was something so mysterious and leading about his eyes, almost as if I could see right to his heart and he made direct eye contact with me causing me to blush instantly.

"Lauren my name is Lauren" I said

"Nice to meet you Lauren, You're very hard to get with"

"Wait, have we met?"

"No, not officially but ever since I saw you I made it my business to get to know you and I take it you received my flowers?'

"How did you know where I lived, are you some kind of stalker?"

"Naw sweetie just a powerful guy there isn't much in my city that I don't have access to" he said smiling.

"You kinda hurt my feelings turning my drinks down a few weeks ago you know that's not polite"

"Oh so you were behind that as well. Well I'm sorry Jayson but I don't take to lightly to someone having so much access to me cause I'm not the average girl?" I said a little flattered.

"I don't mean to be rude but can we go talk in private?" he asked.

Something in my mind told me to turn him down but there was something about him that I wanted to know. His eyes just told a story that I would only know by talking to him.

I followed him to a well lit hallway in the club wondering where he was taking me but I just followed. I noticed an elevator and I had to ask at that point.

"Umm where are we going" I said puzzled

"My office" he replied.

"Your office" I questioned

"Yes my office, I own this club" he said so nonchalant

It was in that very moment I decided he was someone I needed to know. We approached his office, which overlooked the club, but from club level you could not see inside it looked like a big glass mirror. He offered me a drink and sat across from me on the chair. We began to talk for what seemed like hours because the lights in the club came on and the DJ was telling the crowd goodnight and get home safe.

"Sorry, I have to cut or conversation short I know my cousin Shay is looking for me" I stated

He walked me back to the main area in the club and I spotted Shay.

"Bitch I been looking all over for you all night" she sounded pissed.

"I'm sorry I was talking to um um Jayson" I said to Shay clearly she was worried.

Shay and Jayson looked at each and said what's up it was clear they knew each other. Shay said she would meet me at the car.

"Let me walk you to your car" said Jayson

"It's fine I'm a big girl plus I don't want to ruffle the feathers of any of these chicks you may mess with. I'm sure they are here watching" I said.

"If I did have a girl I would not be standing here talking to you ma" he replied.

"Ummm Hmm" I said sarcastically.

We walked to the car and I can tell he was impressed with how I was riding.

"This you?" He said

"This is me" I replied

"Nice, so when will I able to talk to you again?" Handing me is phone obviously wanting my number.

I took his phone stored my number and I guess it's safe to say that the rest was history.

CHAPTER 2

Jayson

I don't know what it was about shorty but she had my attention. I'm not into all the chasing shit I mean I'm that nigga I don't chase bitches cause they always around but these hoes just looking for a come up. Don't let the street shit fool you cause I'm a lovey dovey type of nigga

I just need me a grown ass woman that I can trust and spoil to death with time, love and money of course. I'm getting older and that different bitch every night shit was getting old and these bitches think they got so much game.

Miss Lauren had something about her that I wanted to explore and it made it 100% better that she was not one of these chicks from around the way but I did wonder what she was doing here all the way from Charlotte and she said she graduated law school from NYC so what was she running from. Oh well I planned on really getting too know her so I'd figure out what was really good.

Business was good that night at the club but that was the usual. When I finally headed back up to my office from grabbing the deposit from the bar my man KP was up already waiting for me.

"What's up my G?" I gave KP a pound.

"Tonight was good. Homeboy brought all the bitches out for his b-day and the bottles was flowing all around I had to go get some Moet and Henny out of the stock so make sure you have Kesh grab some extra when she make the liquor inventory" said KP

"Oh but who was ole girl you was rapping to all night?"

"Man I don't even know shorty she just moved here from out of town but I seen her before. Something about her I like" I said rubbing my chin.

"She easy on the eyes my nigga" said KP

"Tell me about it" I said.

"But anyways what was the figure from downstairs?"

"$70,260.00" enough to make that deposit so we can handle that other business" I said

"Fo sho" KP slammed his shot and walked out the door.

KP was my right hand and the only muthafucka that I trusted besides Mac. I mean just that but when you come from where I come from you don't trust nobody. But KP that's my brother from another mother, we been down since the sandbox literally way before all the money and shit we was just in and out the juvenile detention centers. He was like the brother I never had and we been through it all together and nothing has changed except we got some real paper now.

Form the trenches of the street we built an empire and now we co own one of the biggest nightclubs in the city along with a few carwashes, laundry mats and corner stores. All in route to my exit from the streets. This drug shit wasn't what it used to be. Often I look at my surroundings and I still can't believe how far I made it.

Damn I think back to just being a young nigga on the block really too damn young to be out there with the vultures but I was determined to get a dollar by any means possible. Nobody was willing to give me shit so fuck it I had to get up and go get it myself.

Only nigga I had was KP we used to hustle from sunup to sunup somedays. We weren't sleeping, eating, fucking or none of that shit we was just getting money. I made my first 10 bands at like 16 that was a lot of money back then I thought I was ballin but I still wanted more. But I can never forget taking my first of many losses on my way to the top.

See back when I got in the game it was still rules and codes to the streets. We respected our old heads and you respected other mfs territory don't get me wrong we had beef and shit but it wasn't nothing like this weird shit see today. These young niggas now ain't in it for the money they want the bitches and the fame and that's the absolute worst part of the game. But anyways I used to hide my money from day to day outside my window behind this brick. See nobody knew in my house that I had started getting a little money but like I said before they couldn't be trusted so I wouldn't dare keep anything in the house. My plan was smooth each day I'd put my money there and at the end of the week when I went to grandma's house to spend the night I would take all the money and hide it in her basement. That was my safe spot or at least that's what I thought. That Friday night I took my money from the week which was about 2G's. I already had about $3,400 saved at grandma's house. I knew my next flip would be big and I would really start getting some money. See my philosophy was "more dope more money" I would go all in on my packs and I always had more profit then the other niggas that wanted to nickel and dime on their re ups.

It was my Uncle G's birthday so all my family was at my grandma house. It was a slow night so I decided to go kick it with the family and chill. By the time I made it all them muthafuckas was pissy drunk and talking shit. No one was in the basement so I knew I was in the clear to put up my money from the day. Immediately I knew something was off I was so detailed in how I put shit and it was not how I left it. I went up to the tile in the ceiling and it was slightly pushed up that right there sent so many red flags I pushed that bitch in and reached for the small duffle bag that my money was in when I pulled it out my shit was completely empty. I was so fucking pissed I was just about to storm up the stairs and fuck everyone up but that would have been off impulse I was too calculated for that. I acted as if nothing happened I knew that whoever stole my shit would start acting like a muthafucka that got a little money and then that's when I would fuck them up.

For the next few days I paid close attention everyone's moves. I knew it wasn't my grandma cause she would never steal from anyone but come to find out it was the one person I thought I could trust more than anything my fucking MOTHER sad part is how could I harm my mother ? I was so mad and hurt till this day I don't think she knows that I know she stole from me, but from that day forward it put a strain on our relationship. It did more mental damage because it fucked up my ability to trust a woman. Shit if I can't trust my own momma then I know a random bitch would get out on me in a heartbeat.

Lauren

Wow he really had me wide open he was so romantic everything he did seemed to be so well thought out. I haven't liked someone this much in so long. We talked everyday all day he texts me just to let me know he is thinking of me, he texts me to see how my day is going and he is always the one it initiate a date. He was doing all this and a bitch hadn't even given up the goodies. Geesh I found myself daydreaming about his fine ass and how corny and giggly I got in his presence like a little ass girl all over again.

My office phone rang I knew it was my receptionist Nikki

"Yes Nikki" I answered

"It's your mother on line 2" Nikki said

"Thank you Nik, I got it" I said with suspicion because mommy never calls my office.

~ 40 ~

"Hey mommy, what's up?" I said always happy to hear from the queen.

"Well hello darling, I don't want to keep you just wanted you to know we are giving your brother a birthday party and you have to be here, Oh and bring that man I hear has been sweeping you off your feet" she laughed.

"Oh mom what are….."

Before I could finish she said on baby I gotta go this is your Aunt Pam on the other line. I love you and see you soon. Bye. Click.

I just stared at the phone and smiled. I was gonna kick Shay ass because no one told her to run her damn mouth about nothing. Damn. I liked him and all but to bring him around my family and especially my overprotective ass brothers and my messy messy sister. Maybe I can just say he had business and couldn't make it. But knowing my mom she would not buy that answer.

But one thing for sure I couldn't miss Jamie's birthday party for anything in the world although it's been so long since I been home. Me and Jayson have dinner plans later so maybe I'll bring it up then and see what he thinks but first things first I was gonna get miss loud mouth Shay.

I finished up my work for today and straightened up my office like I did any other day and headed for the door. Everyone had gone home for the day but I had stayed a few extra hours because I had my first major case coming up and I needed to be on point. I got to my car threw on my shades and hit the sunroof. I loved my rides home from work because I would just drive, no music just me and my thoughts. I had come a long way and I worked so very hard to be exactly where I was in my life. Everything was going well and I was blessed.

.

My phone always seemed to interrupt my thoughts but an instant smile came across my face because it was my boo.

"Hey Beautiful" he said soon as I answered the phone.

"Hello handsome" I replied

"Just making sure I was still picking you up around 8 for dinner baby. I been waiting to see you all day" he asked.

"Yes I will be ready I'm headed home now to get ready." I said.

"Cool. See you in a little beautiful" Jayson said

I hung up the phone blushing so hard. Thinking about how sexy I had to look for dinner. He always picked the best restaurants and I had to look stunning.

Once I got home I headed straight to my closet and picked on a tight fitting blush dress and some strappy high heels very simple and classy but showed all my curves just enough to have him looking at my ass all night long. It was 6:45pm so I had to move quickly because this man was always on time. I hopped in the shower and got ready. My blowout was already perfect and I caught on to how much Jayson liked my real hair. Just a pinch of eyeshadow and I was gorgeous in record time. Like always Jayson was outside on time but he always came to my door to get me. When I opened the door he was standing there looking so good in his Armani button down and tailored pants and smelling good enough to get me out my panties right here right now if I was wearing some. He looked me up and down and licked his full smooth lips, he reached in to pull me in for a nice tight hug he cupped my ass just a little and I didn't even mind. I was ready to skip dinner and take him in the house and make magic.

"You look absolutely beautiful." he said releasing me from his embrace.

He grabbed my hand and led me to the car as always he opened the door and helped me get in always such a gentleman. On the ride to the restaurant, we talked about each other's day and some other small talk. My mind was focused on exactly how I would ask him to come to the birthday party with me. We pulled up to La'Blue some fancy restaurant in the downtown area close by the water. The waiter seated us outside alone which I am pretty sure was a part of his charming little plans. It was so peaceful and calm you could hear the water and the light breeze that felt so good against my skin and through my hair. I felt so sexy as I sat in front of him. He had this way of looking at me as if he had seen a goddess. We ordered our drinks and food as we waited his phone rang I knew it had to be important because he excused himself to take the call. Naturally I couldn't help but wonder what could interrupt our date because he never answered his phone

really when we spent time together he always said it
could wait.

He came back to the table our drinks had arrived.
As bad as I wanted to ask I didn't I just waited to see
what he would say. He apologized and carried on like
normal. I didn't want to make big deal out of nothing plus
he wasn't my man why was I even trippin in the inside.
I began to tell him that in a few weeks I would be going
out of town.

"Where are you going you didn't ask me" He said
smiling

"I didn't know I needed permission sir" I laughed

"Nah I'm playing where you headed" he said.

"I'm going home to visit it's my big brother's birthday
and he is having a big party"

"Oh" he said

"Why you say it like that?' I asked

"I figured we been going so hard you would be ready for me to meet the fam"

"You would want to come? Honestly I was going to ask I didn't know how you would feel"

"Of course I would come only if you really want me to. I fuck with you I would love to see this beautiful mother you always talk so highly of" he said.

"Well I guess I should book two flights and two hotel rooms"

"Don't worry about none of that I will handle it. Just worry about what the only thing you woman care about anyways" he said

"And what is that" I laughed.

"The perfect outfit so you can kill it as you would say" We both laughed so hard. I didn't admit it but that was exactly what was on my mind.

I was secretly excited that he wanted to meet my family but what did this mean for us? I wasn't looking for him to be my man and I wasn't tryna be his girl. We had this very cool vibe to our relationship that I was not willing to compromise just by adding a title. I liked what we were doing and how it was being done. I don't need none of that extra shit right now. After all I didn't even know what the dick was like but the way shit seems to be going I'm sure I would find out soon.

Once our food came we began to eat my food was so delicious the lemon pepper cream sauce that was over my chicken had to be the most flavorful thing I had in a long time.

"You always pick the best spots to eat" I complimented

"Growing up I couldn't afford to eat good so I told myself when I got some money I would make it my business to eat at the best restaurants. Plus a nigga like to eat but I love some home cooked meals" he said

"Well I am sure you will get enough of them when we visit my mom she loves to feed people especially guests, that when she really start showing out."

"Uh oh am I dating the wrong woman?" he laughed

"She is a mess. Oh dating, so that's what we are doing?" I said

Jayson just stared at me with the same look as always. Seemed as though he wanted to say something but he held back. Once dinner was over we headed out valet had pulled his car around and we headed back to my house. I had to be up super early this case was killing me. When we pulled in my driveway I truly didn't want the night to end but Jayson hopped out and open the car door for me, grabbing my hand slowly walking me to my door. When we reached the door I unlocked it.

"Goodnight beautiful" Jayson said. He leaned in to give me a kiss on the forehead and give me a hug.

"Goodnight. I'll call you in the morning" Closing the door but secretly wishing he was staying the night. He was becoming something so amazing in my life. There was never a dull moment between us we always laughed, joked and talked about so much. We were both beginning to open up about things that we would normally keep a secret. The more I learn about his struggle the more I respect his will and drive. He was the definition of self-made and although he kept most of his business dealing way from me, I still understood. See I knew this present day Jayson but I was always curious to learn about the Jayson before making it. Just the thought of him made moist and it was only matter of time before I would explode. My body was craving for his attention because each time we were together my pussy did a little tingle. I would make sure to get close to him on this little getaway to NC.

I headed into work that morning and Justice my paralegal was already waiting in my office with the files I needed for the day. Justice was a very hard worker I liked her because she was young and she was not compromising her morals to get ahead she was like a mini version of myself. We had been working around the clock on this case. It was my first big case and I needed a slam-dunk if I wanted the name in this town and I really wanted to boost my clientele. This murder case would help elevate my career as an attorney. So innocent or guilty that didn't matter I needed to get him off and that exactly what I planned on doing.

"Thanks Justice" I said

"Everything is here, all the records and history but either homeboy is not who the streets have him to be or he's

just really smart because he has only been in trouble once as a juvenile," Justice said.

"That's great for us the D.A is trying to push Murder 1 and we cannot let that happen. I'll double check the tapes to see if I can see anything different." I said pouring my cup of coffee.

" On another note and off the record, ummmm you've been walking around here doing a lot of smiling and it starting to look like funeral home in here with all these flowers you've been gettiing, so who is this mystery man? " Justice laughed.

"See first off nosey why I gotta be smiling because of a man?" I said

"Well I hope it's not a girl" she teased

"Only a man can bring that kind of glow" Justice said.

"You so nosey, if you must know his name is Jayson" I said smiling.

Before Justice could ask any more questions Nikki rang the intercom.

"Hey Lauren there is someone here to see you can I send them in?" Nikki said

"Yes send them back" I replied

Justice got up to walk out and as she opened the door my smile got even wider. There he was standing at the door with this huge ass box.

"Speaking of the devil" Justice mumbled.

"Um Jayson this Justice, Justice this is Jayson" I introduced them.

"Nice to meet you Justice. I've heard lots about you" Jayson extended his hand giving Justice a firm handshake.

"Nice to meet you also, I wish I could say the same" she smile and walking out the door.

I shook my head and laughed I would get her later on.

"What brings you by" I asked

"This beautiful lady standing in front of me" Jayson

replied.

"What a nice surprise" I grabbed the box off my desk

"I assume this is for me?" I questioned.

As he sat on the couch Jayson, he began to look around

my office with admiration. His eyes were fixed on the

three degree that hung on the wall behind my desk.

"So this is where all the magic happens," he said.

"This is it my second home" I laughed.

"Beauty and Brains" he just smiled.

"Open your gift" he said.

I opened the box only to see a smaller box so I opened

that box and there was an even smaller box.

"Oh you got jokes" I said.

Finally, I got to a white envelope with my name on it.

Inside were two plane tickets dated for May 12th and

returning on May 18th going to Montego Bay, Jamaica.

"What's this" I questioned

"Well you do have birthday coming up I figured we could

get away since you don't know many people here

anyways" Jayson said.

"But my birthday is not for another month, why are you

telling me so early?"

"Honestly babe it's kinda a peace offering because some

business came up and I won't be able to come with you to

your brother's party. I am so sorry. Are you mad?" He

asked.

"Mad? No. A little bummed. Yes." I said.

"But since you come with an alternative I will forgive

you" I gave him a hug and accepted the offer to go to

Jamaica.

"Great, I can't wait to get you alone on the beach" he said in my ear.

"Call me when you get a chance later, I gotta run"

"Ok."

Just like that, he was out the door and secretly I was curious to know what had come up so sudden but then again I was relieved that I would not get the 3rd degree from my brothers. I am sure its club business anyways I told myself.

Justice walked in my office "Soooo you did not tell me you were seeing Jayson Black" she said in a high pitch voice.

"Honestly I didn't know my personal business was up for discussion nosey" I said.

"Well Jayson Black my dear is not just anyone around here everyone knows that but if your boujee ass wasn't being so secretive you would've known that?" Justice walked away sticking her tongue out.

All this Jayson Black talk was distracting me from my work so I began to prepare my opening statements for this trial once this "W" was on my record and I made a name for myself in this city I would then begin to do a little more homework on my new found love interest. Rereading and writing my notes I just knew that the state would not be able to meet their burden of proof and with the proper talk game my client would walk away a free man. There are just way too many holes I thought to myself. The day had past when I looked at the clock it was 6:15pm I had truly worked the day away without any disruption and I was grateful. By now I was starving and I had done more than enough work in the office. If anything else came up I could just do it at home. I called for Justice and she was already getting ready to head out herself but now was the perfect time to pick her brain a

little about Jayson.

"You getting out of here for the day" I said

"Yes girl, I think you're going to win this case Lauren"

said Justice.

"Believe me I hope so that would help get me some more

clients for sure" I replied. "But anyway when you said

that Jayson Black isn't just anyone what did you mean?"

I quizzed.

"Girl, He is NOT your average nigga the whole city

knows him. He used to be the biggest connect on the east

coast. Managed to never get caught and was smart

enough to turn his street royalty into many successful

businesses. He a legit self-made boss. Like the shit you

read in the books. Yes, that's him in the flesh. Plus, he

doesn't have a bunch of kids with a bunch of woman and

just trifling. I'm sure he is a typical nigga and got bitches but his shit is not all over the streets he is a very private person. And I hear he has this big ass mansion on the upper side of town that sits off the water. I know he has a baby momma with one daughter and they were together like 8 years or some shit but I don't think that's his girl anymore. Rumor is he got her living nice too downtown in a penthouse condo. The daughter is like 15 or 16 I think, she's a basketball player all in the newspaper and shit.

Well damn I thought to myself she sure knows an awful lot about such a private person but I guess it's true that the street definitely talk around here. Shit back in Charlotte all this information would get a person lined up. I guess they just move different here.

Justice was still talking but I had not heard a word she said just processing all the information she has just rambled.

"Thanks boo" I said I had heard all I needed for now I'm sure she would have plenty more when the time was right.

"Of course, but Lauren overall he is really a nice guy I think and yawl mad cute. Did you see how he was looking at you? It was pure admiration. He never had a woman like you" She said.

"Thanks" I smiled.

"We out of here. See you tomorrow" She got in her Benz put on her shades and headed out the parking garage.

I got in my car and headed home. Thinking that I left Charlotte getting away from all the drug life and now I'm here dating another drug dealer. Great. Just Great.

If he is as big as they say he is then I'm just hoping that he and my brother are not already affiliated. They would never go for me dating someone they did business with. It's like they always want to protect me from niggas like themselves. I know all about what it's like to date a real boss I watched my momma do it all her life, the late nights, business trips, stress and worry. The only difference is my daddy was a real OG he didn't work the streets and he didn't cheat on my mom and put her through all that dumb shit. It was just the life and I had seen it firsthand. Up until this point Jayson had been honest with me about his life well the little I has inquired about but I guess it was time for me to truly get to know this man that had the ability to make me weak just from his smile and I planned on doing just that.

CHAPTER 3

Jayson:

"Hey baby girl, wake up" pushing Mariah gently.

"Good Morning Daddy" she woke smiling.

Mariah is my baby. My 16-year-old gem, nothing and absolutely nothing moves if she doesn't approve of it. The day she was born was the day I started to transition from street to business. She is my everything, beautiful smart and one hell of a ball player.

"Why, I gotta get up dad, I don't have practice and I could have stayed at mom's to be up all early" she laughed.

"Let's get some breakfast I kinda want to talk to you about something" I said.

"Ok cool, let me get cute" she kissed my cheek and jumped up.

I laughed, that girl is such a clown but I hope she would be feeling what I had to say.

"Ah, dad" Mariah peeked from the bathroom door brushing her teeth.

"Yes, baby"

~ 62 ~

"So this afternoon we still having our one on one session" she said.

"You know I'm not missing an opportunity to win against a superstar" I said.

Every Saturday my baby and I have a little one on one basketball game in our home gym just to keep her tight and on her game. It's something we been doing ever since she picked up a basketball.

"I'll be in the kitchen, what we eating?" I said

"Whatever is cool dad" she replied.

I always kept my fridge stocked so it was no problem to whip us up something quick. Eggs, turkey bacon, pancakes and some fruit. I enjoy cooking something I wish I had more time to do but in due time I would be all the way out the streets and able to be 100% a family man.

"Smells good" Mariah sang coming in the kitchen.

We sat at the table and began to eat and buss it up. See I had a real relationship with my baby. She knew what she needed to know about my life but I didn't hide anything from her that could potentially cause her harm later down the line. She knew her dad was someone important and she knew that it was equally important for her to live by my instructions. She was privileged and even more spoiled being an only child on top of being a great kid. We had a bond that I could not explain. I trusted her and she trusted me. Although her mom and I did not work out, she never once chose her mom's side over mines. She loved both of us equally and she never once told mom anything we would talk about. This was my dawg and she kept it so real with her dad.

"So what's up dad? What's on your mind?" she asked

"You know I tell you all my secrets, Right?" I said.

"Right, so spill it who is she?" said Mariah

I looked puzzled "Who is she?" I laughed.

"Yes, who is she, daddy you know I know you like the back of my hand, you been smiling a lot and in your phone. You never even have your phone that much well not your personal phone at least" she said

I just laughed she was my daughter for real always observant and aware of what was going on around her.

"Well, you kind of right there is someone, but I don't know Riah" I said

"Well, it's something if you're telling me because you haven't talked about any other woman to me other than mom. Who is she?" she asked again.

"That's the point, I don't know her that much. She's new in town from North Carolina, She's an attorney her name is Lauren" I replied.

"An attorney? Well that's good she's certainly not ratchet and after your money so that's a plus" she laughed.

"Yeah we been talking for awhile, she cool, interesting" I said.

"Sounds to me like you like her daddy, you know I want you to be happy. Do you plan on being in a relationship with her?" Mariah asked.

"I don't know. I want to get to know her more and I want you to meet her and because you know if you don't like her than it's probably not going to work seeing how you're my #1 girl" I said.

"Well I would say invite her to my game on Wednesday but you know mommy be trippin. I wish she get her something to do," We both laughed.

"Yeah, I'm not ready for your mom's shit" I said.

"How about after my game she meets us for dinner?" said Mariah

"Yeah, I'll ask her" I said.

It was a relief that Mariah was cool meeting Lauren. She has been on my mind heavy. I have not felt like this since when I first met my baby mom Taylor. I remember the feeling she gave me when I first seen her. Taylor was beautiful, smart and different. We had been through a lot of shit and she held me down through a lot of this street shit. I took Taylor through the most but I was young and dumb with more money then I knew what to do with and that always brought bitches and problems. We had just finally grew apart and after 8 years we had now been separated going on 3 years but every now and then Taylor would start her bullshit and want to have drama with me. I feel like I owe her for all the shit I put her through so I pay all her bills and paid off her cars. Mariah's car is also paid for of course and I handle her insurance and shit too. I also put money in her account monthly but now I'm ready to move on and be in a relationship shit I want a

wife. But on the other hand I'm not ready for the drama
that I know Taylor is going to bring. She says that she is
over me but I know she damn sure is not going to want to
see me be the man she always wanted me to be with
another woman.

"Oh dad, it's nice to see you smiling" Mariah said
snapping me out of my thoughts.

"Thanks gorgeous. Now let's go get this work" I kissed
her on her forehead. We headed downstairs to the gym
and began our game.

Now that I got my time in with my baby girl, it was time
to get to business and make sure everything was
everything. I realized it was 2pm and I had not talked to
Miss Lauren all day so I Face Timed her. Like always,
she answered looking so fresh and gorgeous like she had
just took a shower. I appreciated that she wasn't caked
up with makeup and always dolled up she was

comfortable with her natural beauty and her lips, damn her lips were perfect and she always kept them perfectly glossed.

"Well good afternoon handsome" she smiling into the camera.

"Hello beautiful" I replied.

"How has your Saturday been?" she asked.

"It's been great. I played basketball with my daughter hence why I'm headed to shower now and get ready for my day" I replied

"Awe that's sweet, did she beat you? And don't lie." She laughed.

"I let her win," I laughed back.

"Sure you did, I heard she's pretty nice on the court" she said.

"She is. One day you will have to come check her out" I said.

"As long as there is an invitation I most certainly will, I always secretly wished I could play basketball but don't tell nobody" she said placing her finger to her lips.

"Secret safe with me" I said.

"Cool" she laughed.

"So when can I see you busy lady" I asked.

"You know people make time for what they want and for you I can work something into my schedule" She said. We both laughed. It was nice that we had the ability to just joke and laugh. We both always seemed to smile whenever we talked. Just a real down to earth chick. Not trying to impress me and not all up in my pockets. She was the perfect reflection of a boss. I liked that, I liked her.

"Well it's the weekend so how about today" I asked.

"Sure. I'm taking a small break from work this weekend since I've been preparing for this case so hard. I'm going to go do a little shopping and I should be free later. What time were you thinking?" She asked.

"I'll have to see you in action, I bet you're a sassy ass lawyer" I teased.

"I am" she laughed.

"9 o'clock?" I said

"Sounds good to me" she replied.

"If you think something you want to do just shoot me a text, talk to you later beautiful" I hung up.

I showered and headed out the door to this meeting with Mac and KP we had to check out this new spot that could potentially be our next business. It was a beautiful sunny day. Days like this made me appreciate all the struggle I had been through to get to this point. I pushed my 550 Benz down my long drive way and started my day. I pulled up to the building and my niggas were already there waiting. We did a walk through with the female realtor and immediately we signed the paper work to buy the building. This would eventually be a strip club. Once we handled the business with that building it was now time to make sure this meeting in Mexico next week went flawless as usual.

"So you flying out Monday" KP asked.

"Yes, then yawl coming down Tuesday" I said

"Well this drop right here is the most important because of the little bullshit war they having" Mac said.

"Hell yeah 200 of them, just in case shit goes left with them Mexicans" I added.

"Juan guaranteed nothing will change even though they at war but I rather be safe than sorry cause ya'll know I plan on leaving this shit alone for good next month." I said.

"Yeah nigga we know," They both said at the same time.

Aye, yo so the little shorty you was talking to at the club the other night. I hear she is this new attorney for that

Jones firm downtown and shit. They say she nice too. I heard she was representing the nigga Rashaad on that murder case." Mac said

"Oh yeah" I replied.

"Yeah, you might've hit the jackpot G" KP said.

"Shit we gonna see, I like shorty" I said.

"Yeah until Taylor kill your ass" Mac laughed.

"This nigga know damn well Taylor gonna be with the fuck shit soon as she find out" They dapped each other laughing.

"That shit ain't funny, it's a fucking headache," I said.

"You already know your baby mom crazy and I fuck with T she gonna be thinking I got something to do with it nigga and you know that's gonna have my household in a fucking uproar" said KP.

"Nigga I didn't tell you to start dating her homie and plus you a grown ass man you better not let my shit control your house." I said.

"You better be ready for the shit and just hope shorty can ride that wave. We all know Taylor crazy as fuck." said Mac.

"I got this, worry about ya own shit. I'm out." I laughed dapped them both and head back to the crib to pick Mariah up so she could go get her car cleaned. I would stop down by the boat on the way and make a reservation for later.

Laruen:

My Saturday cleaning was all finished, I had been ahead of the game with this case, and now it was time to do a little retail therapy. I worked hard and shopped even harder. Well every woman in my family had a bad shopping habit. The joke is daddy worked so hard because we shopped so much. Although I don't need anything to wear tonight, I'm sure I would pick something up just in case. It's such a nice day reminds me of back home. On the ride to the mall I called my mom just to check on her, I miss her.

"Hey mommy" I said into the phone.

"Hey baby, how are?" she said.

"I'm good just working hard"

"That's great you ready for the case to be over?"

"Yes. Mommy but I'm ready you know I've waited my whole life to get in that courtroom." I said.

"I know and you know daddy would be so proud of you" said mom.

"I know mommy, what you doing though?" I asked.

"Girl nothing, the kids are coming to stay the night later you know your brother Jamie call himself having a new girlfriend" she gossiped. We both laughed.

"What's wrong with my kids?" she said.

"Mommy you know they are a mess," I said.

"Well make sure you call and get the info, you know they tell you more than they will tell me and London," she said.

"Where she at anyways" I asked.

"She should be stopping by any minute to drop off the new deed for my space for the boutique."

"I'm proud of you mom for doing something you love and not always putting our stuff before what you want to do" I said.

"Thanks baby, I'm excited." She said.

"And you know you have to plan the grand opening"

"Of course: I replied.

"I think that's London pulling up now I hear that damn music," she said.

"That girl ain't never going to change, daddy used to yell at her all the time like we live in the ghetto" I laughed.

"No home training" mommy laughed too.

"I'm putting you on speaker," she said.

"Hey tramp" said London.

"Hey hey" I replied.

"I miss you sister" said London.

"I miss you too pooh" I replied. Only I could call her pooh.

"I hear you got a man down there that got that ass smiling from Erie to Charlotte," She teased.

"Now see ya'll all talk too dang much, he is not my man just a friend. Dang mommy you tell everyone." I said.

"Everyone except your crazy over protective brothers" London said.

"You better stop letting them run your damn life, they do what the hell they want to and they stay with a new one" London laughed.

"Girl, I don't have time to argue with them two you know they think they are daddy. Anything I say goes in one hear and out the other. I am the baby and that is how they see it. And I'm grown as hell." I laughed.

"Well keep sneaking and you know when they find out they gonna be all in they feelings" said mommy.

"I know, if it gets too serious then I will tell" I said.

"Oh hush I hear the door" said mommy.

"What up" I heard Kyree say.

"Heyyyyyyy brother" I yelled.

"Oh yawl talking to my baby" he said. I could feel his smile through the phone.

"I miss all ya'll so much" I cannot wait to come home for the party.

"We miss you more" They all chimed.

"Oh Lauren call me later got some legal papers for the business I need you to look over" Kyree said.

"Ok. I will call soon as I'm home. Love ya'll. I'm about to go in the mall" I said.

"Some things never change" he laughed. "ya'll all got that shopping shit bad, man even your nieces got it bad and they only kids" he laughed.

"Boy Bye." I said

"Love you, bye" They replied.

It was times like Saturday mornings I missed being at home. We all never planned to go see mommy at the same time but it seemed to always happen. Then our whole day would be gone cause we just bullshitted all day with each other. I miss my siblings and could not wait to go home for a visit.

Finally, I made it to the mall it was already 4pm so I needed to have enough to time to shop and get home so I could see my boo later. I headed into Sax Fifth there was these new Gucci sandals that I just had to have. I walked up to the shoes and there was very pretty young lady with the same sandals I was looking for in her hand.

"Great taste sweetie" I said.

"She turned around and said yes they are so pretty right"

"Very" I said.

"The lady went to get my size so she should be right back" the young girl said.

The woman returned and I asked for my size she handed the young lady her size and she waved bye.

You're very pretty by the way" she said walking away.

"You are gorgeous yourself. Enjoy your sandals I am sure you will wear them well. Have a good day" I said back.

It was such pleasure to see respectful young ladies and she was such a very pretty girl. I remember being her age and buying things that my friends could not afford. She is lucky. I'm sure her parents were not too far. Once the woman cashed me out for my shoes I went and found me some cute sunglasses too match and they had the cutest Gucci T-shirt that I could wear with some shorts for simple look. I didn't need much more but I browsed around a few more stores and grabbed a few things. I had to get me a smoothie on the way out the door and my day would be complete. I would just stop and get a quick Pedi and Mani and head home to get dressed.

My phone buzzed. It was a text.

Jayson: Hey love

Me: Hello. How's it going?

Jayson: Good, Can't wait to see you. We are gonna do something fun so you don't have to wear heels tonight. Lol.

Me: Sounds great. Oh Boy. Should I be nervous?

Jayson: Not at all. I know you tired of all these formal ass dinners we been having just wanna do something more chill.

Me: Ok. See you soon. I'm heading home if a few.

Jayson: K. I'm grabbing my daughter from the mall. I took her car to get cleaned so I guess I'm playing chauffeur until its done. Lol.

Me: That's sweet. Since you washing cars how about mines lol.

Jayson: You should've said something that's nothing to do.

Me: Oh I was just joking I got it covered. Lol

Jayson: Well excuse me Miss Boss. I know you all independent but you know I can lighten some on that manual labor for you.

Me: Thank You.

Jayson: You smiling?

Me: I am. Always these days.

Jayson: That makes two of us then. Lol. See you in a few. I come pick you up.

Me: Okay.

I guess I picked the perfect outfit for my date. I'm kinda glad to be comfortable and not dressed up I kinda just want to chill and watch movies but I guess those dates will come soon enough. The nail salon was not that busy which was great and I could be in and out. I'll get my usual Fire Engine Red and call it a day. The woman hooked my nails and feet up quickly and I was on my way. I was making good time it was only 7pm. Once home I ran my bath and laid my clothes out to press them. I wouldn't take long because I didn't need any makeup I planned on throwing this hair into a pretty ponytail and being super cute and super simple. I always needed to listen to my Jeezy to get me pumped. I poured my glass of wine and began washing up. Nice and clean I applied my new bath and body works lotion all over and sprayed my Bombshell Perfume. I wore a brand new black bra and some sexy black lace boy shorts. Looking in the mirror I admired my body and just how soft and shiny my skin was and smiled. I knew I had it going on and I had no problem putting that shit on just to top it off. I grab my clothes got dressed and did a double look to make sure it was perfect. My new Gucci sandals looked so nice with the shirt and my ponytail was just enough. I hoped I wasn't too relaxed looking. This was definitely a

change from the tight shit Jayson is used to seeing or my
work clothes.

I heard the doorbell and looked at the clock it was
8:43pm. I smiled because this man is never a minute late
or has me waiting. I wasn't quite ready so I just went to
open the door.

Hey, babe come in I'm just about ready" I said opening
the door.

"It's cool do your thing I'm kinda early" he said smiling.

"Be right back" I began walking away and turned around
briefly just as I thought he was watching my ass. I
laughed.

"I just have to change my purse can't be wearing all this
Gucci and carrying my LV bag" I yelled from my room.

"Yeah don't want the boujee committee to kick you out,"
he laughed.

"Shut up, you always got jokes" I said.

I did on last keep in the mirror and when I went to the living room Jayson was so intrigued my painting on my wall over my fireplace to even notice I was standing behind him. Honestly I just stood there starring.

Something so intoxicating took over my body just from his mere presence.

Umm mm" I cleared my throat.

He turned around and was instantly taken back as if he has seen something he never seen before.

"You look so cute" he said.

"Cute. Cute is for puppies" I laughed.

He laughed so hard.

"What am I going to do with you" he said

"I don't know you tell me" I said.

He moved closer and grabbed me palming my ass and kissing me intensely. The air got thick everything got hot.

His soft hand caressed the small of my back and I was melting.

Suddenly he stopped and stepped back just smiling at me.

"Miss Young if we don't leave now I think it's safe to say your pretty little outfit is going to be all over the floor" he smiled.

"That might not be half bad" I mumbled.

"You ready gorgeous, this should be fun" He said.

"Ready as I'll ever be" I replied.

I grabbed my glasses and like that we were out the door. I noticed that each time he picked me up he drove a different car. I admired his 550 Benz similar in color to the one my mom drove. I was hoping that I would get the opportunity to ask him some more about his life.

CHAPTER 4

Jayson:

Damn she is truly gorgeous, and she got a little swag I see. I thought to myself. I reached over and grabbed her hand. I hope she's not afraid of water.

"What you thinking about" I asked.

"What you mean" she said

"You look like you're thinking and we are halfway to our destination and you haven't really said anything" I replied.

"Oh, sorry I was just checking out the scenery you know I still haven't had a real chance to just see the town between work and spending time with you" she said.

"Oh you know a nigga ain't tryna take all your time" I joked.

"Why not?" she asked.

We locked eyes for a moment and before I could say anything my phone rang. It was Mariah so I answered.

"Hello, hey baby girl what's up? Yeah, that's cool. Your car is in the garage. Just text me let me know your good. It's money in that drawer if you need it. Ok. Love you too. Bye" I said.

"Sorry that was my daughter." I said to Lauren.

"No problem" she said.

But I noticed something in her mood has changed. Not bad. Not good just a shift. She was in her thoughts something I noticed a lot from her. She's a thinker I can tell but I'll figure her out in due time. I already made my mind up that I wanted her around for a while and no matter what I had to do I was ready.

We pulled up to the water where they docked the boat. I rented the whole boat because I really just wanted some privacy.

"Omg this is so beautiful. We don't have water like this back home, well at least not this close" she said.

"Yeah it's a nice touch to this place" I said.

"Something about water makes me feel calm, just relaxed" she said.

We board the boat and I could tell she liked it from her smile. I made her a drink and we sat on the couch and just kicked it for a while. Just talking. She explained her life to me about her father's death and just everything about how she became an attorney. I was more in awe with her although she came from money shorty still had a pretty crazy life. Just shows that money can't buy happiness and it damn sure can't fix all your problems.

For the first time in a long time I had opened up and about things I never really talk about. I wanted to be honest with her I felt like I couldn't lie. See to the streets I'm a retired drug dealer but I had to be real with her and explain that I am transitioning she deserved to know the real. I explained it all and even put her deep about my whole relationship with Taylor and the role I still play in her life financially. Looking at her I couldn't tell what she was thinking and I hope this shit don't turn her off and I lose her.

"I respect your honesty" She said.

"Thank you, I feel you deserve that.' I replied.

"I'm not afraid of your life but you have to understand that I come from that and it's also not beneficial to my career to date a drug dealer." She said.

"See Lauren I understand but let me correct you I'm not a drug dealer, I don't touch drugs at all I haven't in years. I'm the plug. My team depends on me to eat and until I make the proper transition and my connect is comfortable dealing with one of them and not me I can't just fall back" I explained.

"I understand" she said.

"Please just let me show you, I am a business man. That wants a family, a wife and just live peacefully." I said looking directly into her eyes.

"I like you, I can't judge you but I will ask that you keep your personal life far away from my professional life as possible." She said bluntly.

"Agreed. I would never bring harm your way." I said.

"I appreciate that" she replied.

"Another thing, I want you to meet my daughter."

She looks shocked.

"What, why you look like that" I asked.

"I'm just surprised that's all, that a big deal." She said.

"Yeah, that's my world and I just want you two to meet. I want you around for as long as you're willing to stay Lauren" I said.

We both just smiled. And she agreed to meet Mariah.

"Now that we have that out the way let's go up top and see this beautiful water" she said smiling.

"I'll lead the way" I said grabbing her hand.

I lead her to the stairs and allowed her to walk up first. Damn just watching her walk up the stairs had me rock hard. I been being a perfect gentleman so far but I can only imagine what she looks like naked cause she just sexy as fuck and she look so damn soft.

Looking at this water made me realize just how much I was ready to settle down and be with one woman. It was time. I have everything a man could want except a wife. All I was hoping was that I wasn't wrong about Lauren she seemed a little too good to be true. But I'd be a damn fool not to try woman like her just don't come around too often.

Lauren:

"Thank you" I said just starring into the moonlight.

"What are you thanking me for" Jayson said.

"Just, thank you it's been a long time since I've been this happy. Being around you makes me happy" I said.

"The feeling is mutual, I like you I really do and hope we can just continue getting to know each other," he said.

Jayson held me from behind being in his arms just felt so right. He was sparking feelings that I have not felt in such a long time. Something I was actual so scared of feeling.

I had built up this wall around me heart and it seemed to be getting knocked down and that was so frightening. My last relationship was a complete disaster. I was terrified to love a person they way I had loved after my mess of a relationship with Deshawn.

Deshawn was my ex we had been together for 6 years. I met him in my process of moving to NYC for school. He was one of the first people I had met. I could never forget I was lost getting on the subway and he helped me out. From that moment we became friends and he was very very sweet in the beginning. Time had passed and we decided to date. Deshawn was making his way to the top in the streets and by the time we had been in a relationship for about two years he was what the law would consider "kingpin".

We lived very well and I didn't want for anything. Deshawn was supportive of my dreams and me becoming an attorney. He was perfect. Then one-day things began to change. He was very disrespectful and had started putting his hands on me. At first I thought maybe it was just a bad day because he was extremely apologetic and I forgave him. It didn't happen again for about another month and this time was worse than before. Then it happened again and again for no reason at all. If I said something wrong we fought, if I was at the store too long

we fought, shit if the nigga stayed out all night we fought.

Deshawn found a reason to fight me about anything. I

had become so afraid of him and I had no one in NYC

except my friend Tisha and Kya.

If it wasn't for Kya I'd probably be dead. Deshawn had

beaten me up so bad one day. It was so bad that I could

not hide it normally if he hit me I was able to apply some

makeup and no one would notice. This time I had a huge

black eye and a bunch of bruises all over my arms and

my neck from him grabbing and choking me.

Kya had enough she was so pissed when she had come to

my house to bring me notes from missing class. She had

been trying to get me away from Deshawn for years now.

She hated his ass and I promised her I was going to leave

I was just scared.

"I know you are scared of this nigga but you don't have to put up with this shit Lauren" Kya said.

"I know Kya, I'm leaving" I replied.

"well not to through salt on an open wound but what im about to tell you should help you leave this clown much faster" she said.

"What now?" I asked.

"So I was at Mindy's getting my lashes done and this girl named Keisha was in there running her fucking mouth about her nigga just buying her a new car and moving her into a new house up in Queens. So I'm lying in the chair with my back turned to the door bitch you will never guess who the fuck walked in the door and paying for this bitch hair" she said.

I did not even have to answer her because I already knew what she was about to say. I never told Kya but I found out about this bitch Keisha and confronted Deshawn and that why my face looked like this now. But for the sake of not looking like an even bigger fool I just played like I didn't know.

"Please don't say Deshawn," I said.

"Bitch yes, that muthafucka walked in and he never saw me because my back was in the chair but I seen him through the mirror. He paid and they left out like husband and fucking wife. I wanted to get up and fight the bitch but I didn't want to draw in case we needed to build the case more" Kya said.

"I don't even care Kya she can have him, I done saved enough money and I found me a little apartment. I'm moving tomorrow I just don't want his ass to find out where I'm living at all." I said.

"Well let's pack your shit and you can spend the night at my house tonight until tomorrow," said Kya.

I was happy that I had Kya she was a real New York bitch, thorough as they came and never judgmental. That was my bitch. That night I had blocked Deshawn from my cell phone and moved into my place the next day. I was glad to be getting away from his crazy ass for good this time.

A month had passed and I had not heard or seen DeShawn and I was so relieved maybe he just said fuck it and decided to just let me go. I had to go pick my brother Kyree up from LaGuardia Airport today he had some business up here in the city. Thank goodness my damn face was healed because it would be hell for Deshawn if my brother knew about his shenanigans.

I grabbed Kya to ride with me she loved when my brother came up I knew that she low key liked him and I wouldn't put it past him if they had not fucked but I minded my business. She didn't tell, I didn't ask, and I liked it that way. I already had my share of drama between my friends and my brothers.

I made it to the airport just in time Kyree has coming out. I beeped my horn getting his attention.

"Hey brother" giving him a big hug.

"Thanks, for scooping me baby, I missed you," he said kissing my forehead. Kyree always reminded me of daddy. He acted just like him.

"Hey Kya" Kyree said.

They gave each other a long embrace and that was all the conformation I needed that my brother had absolutely smashed Kya before.

"I got you a rental and I'm gonna take your car, we should be able to pick it up now" he said.

"Ok" I replied. I knew better than to get into details in front of Kya. I trusted whatever my brother wanted to do especially when it came to him handling his business.

As we pulled, up to Enterprise, I notice Kyree staring at me but I didn't say anything. I hope that you could not still see my bruises or something.

Kyree followed me to my house so he could put up his bags and shower.

"After I handle things we gonna go have dinner and catch up" Kyree said.

"Good, just come back a scoop me when you done I'll get ready cause I know you hate waiting" I laughed.

About 7 o'clock Kyree texted me saying he was pulling up.

I went outside and we headed to Ruth Chris the NYC one is the best of them all by far. The car ride was very quiet minus a small talk about the kids and how mommy was doing since she lost dad.

Once we got to the restaurant we ordered and Kyree looked me dead in my face.

"You okay Lauren" he said.

"Yes, I'm good bro, happy to see you" I said.

"No, you good up here living alone and shit, your money right?" he asked.

"Yes I am fine, you and Jamie send money every month which is plenty plus I do work " I said smiling.

"I know I just can't have my baby sister up here struggling and shit or depending on that corny ass nigga you dating, what's up with homie you ain't said nothing about him all day," he said.

"Well we been broke up about a month ago, he was cheating" I said.

"Damn, why you ain't say nothing but fuck that nigga it's his loss sis you know that. I always tell you and London that ya'll are Queens and you can't be out here moving like a servant competing with other bitches that not on your level" Kyree said.

"I know that's why I left soon as I found out Ky" I said.

"You know I'm keeping it 100 wit you. I myself ain't shit but that's why I don't got no girl. I'm not ready to settle down or none of that. I put Jackie through the most all cause I wasn't ready and I said I would never do a woman like that again." He said.

"I know, I know that's why I love you because we can talk about anything." I said.

We finished our dinner and headed back to my house.

"I hate when you come for one day," I said to Kyree.

"What time does your fight leave?"

"At 8:30am and you know I only come up here when necessary I hate up North it's too cold." He laughed.

I enjoyed just kicking it with my brother. We watched some tv and fell asleep on the couch. It was about 3am when he woke me up to get in my bed.

Then we both heard this weird ass noise at my window like someone was tryna get in.

"Shhhhhh" Kyree motioned with his hands on his mouth.

I seen him reach for his gun and cocked it.

I stood up against the wall out of his way. All I seen was the shadow coming through the window it was Deshawn.

Before I could even blink all in heard was BOOM, BOOM BOOM, BOOM !!!

I was so scared it was still kinda dark and I couldn't see. I ran to the light.

"OH MY GOD" I said but I don't think the words came out of my mouth.

Deshawn was lying in a pull of blood with a gun in his hand. DEAD!

Kyree took his gun and put it in his waist he told me to go in the room and wait for him. I did exact as I was told . I couldn't believe it. What if my brother was not here?

What if he would have killed Kyree? What if the police is on their way?

My mind was racing at a mile a minute and I was pacing the floor.

I could hear Kyree on the phone but I couldn't make out exactly what he was saying. About 15 minutes passed and I could hear the front door open and then shut. Another 30 minutes had passed and Kyree came in the room he told me to go get in the shower. I did. When I came out the shower there was NO Deshawn, NO blood, NO nothing.

Kyree looked me directly in my eyes grabbing my shoulders. "Nothing happened," he said with extreme sternness in his voice.

"Ok" I said. He hugged me and kissed my forehead.

I dropped Kyree off at the airport at about 8am. He gave me a cell phone and said wait for the call and I would be moving into a new apartment in Manhattan later that day. I gave him a long hug and I knew that everything was okay.

Kyree and I never once ever mentioned Deshawn again somehow I knew that he knew Deshawn has abusing me and I'm sure it came from Kya but I couldn't question her about it. If so I was glad that she did say something. I honestly don't know what happened or what he did with his body. From that day, forward Kyree and I had a bond that was unbreakable. He was my favorite and I would do anything for him because he would do anything for me. Some guy called the phone and came to pick me up he advised I only take my clothes and important papers and pictures.

We pulled up to my new apartment building in Manhattan. It was huge and fully furnished my brother had made sure I would be comfortable and he paid the rent for the entire year. The large floor to ceiling windows provide a view over the entire city of New York, which was a sight that you would have to experience to even understand. The lights gave hope, this city was full of dreams and it was this view that got me through my long nights of studying and my many days of wanting to pack it all up and go back to Charlotte. But I didn't I survived. I never got into another relationship after I just focused on myself but that experience had turned my heart cold. I had trust issues for sure. Therefore, I just threw myself into my work graduated college and law school. I was damn proud of myself. But now I'm here and I have a man that I truly like and seems tobe everything I want. He doesn't know just how fucked up my trust is and even though it's been years I do not want to bring all that baggage into this. Jayson does not deserve that nor does he deserve me not given my all in whatever it is that we have going on. However, when the time comes I am sure we can talk about that. For right now, I will just go with the flow and hope that I don't block my blessing with my ways.

I had vowed that if I ever found love again that he had to be someone I would be sure that my dad would approve of. In his absence that means my brothers have to like him. Everything my gut told me that would not be a problem. Now I just need to make sure this was the real deal and not lust.

We had not spent much time together since our date on the boat and I was so busy with work and getting ready to head home for the birthday party. I was certainly missing my boo and was looking to spending a little quality time in before I left. My week had been crazy trial was near and I was for some reason getting nervous. I knew I had this case in the bag but I was not familiar with any of these judges. I was just a little uneasy but I gave myself a pep talk and shook that shit off quickly.

I could not wait until next week to see my mommy talks with her always helped when I was feeling off about something. She knew exactly what to say to get my fire burning again. Plus, I just needed a little time with her I had to see just how much she knew about what I had going on and secretly I has excited to fill her in about Jayson.

Normally we go out to eat but tonight he had asked if I would come over to his house, and he would cook for me. I loved a man that could cook. Therefore, I was really looking forward to it. I could just relax I did not have to be all dolled up since we weren't going out. A little cuddling after dinner was much needed. I was going to stop home before heading to his house but the day had gotten away from me and it was already 6pm. I did not want to be late for dinner because he is never late. So I finished up and headed out my GPS said his house has about 30 minutes from my office. I decide to text him and let him know I was on my way.

Me: Hey, just wanted to tell you I will be arriving shortly.

Jayson: Great, let me know if you get lost.

Me: Ok, see you soon.

I was in awe when I pulled up to his home. Damn, this nigga is living well I thought. The lawn was cut so precise and neat. I pulled up to the gate and before I could push the button, the gate began to open. I drove up the long driveway and parked.

Jayson met me at the door looking so good of course. He was dressed down in some Nike sweats and a Nike T-shirt. I had never seen him dressed his way and he was so fine. Damn he looked good in anything.

"You made it." he said giving me a big hug.

"Yes, I did and I bought wine because my week oh boy" I laughed.

He took the wine from my hand and took my jacket.

"You look pretty and professional," he said.

"Thanks, I planned on going home and changing but I didn't want to be late" I replied.

"I'm glad you didn't you look like a boss" he smiled.

"I thought my house was nice, you have such a beautiful home"

"Well if you want I can show you around" he said.

He showed me all around and I could not believe that this man lived alone in this big ass 5 bedroom, 3 bathrooms home. Each room was detailed perfectly; his office was so neat and organized. I was in love with the home gym and the basketball court. And lord the kitchen was every woman's dream. The appliances were the best on the market and I was secretly anticipating cooking him a meal in here.

"Make yourself at home" he said. "The food will be done in about 15 minutes; I'll pour you a glass of wine"

"Thank, you." I took off my shoes and got more comfortable.

Then I heard the open and close. Jayson came in with my glass of wine and behind him was a beautiful girl.

"Lauren I'd like you to meet Mariah" he said.

Before I could say anything she reached out for a hug and said "Nice to meet you but I think we've seen each other before."

I looked a little harder and oh my it was the pretty little girl from the Gucci store a few weeks ago in the mall.

"Yes. Hi gorgeous, did you wear your sandals yet?" I asked.

Jayson looked confused. "So what did I miss?" he said.

"Oh daddy remember when I went to the mall and got those Gucci sandals well Lauren was in the store and I asked her opinion and of course I didn't know who she was its just kind of something girls do when we shop. Small world." Mariah said.

"Yes. How ironic" I said.

We all laughed.

"Well I'm going to check on the food and let you two introduce yourselves," he said.

Mariah and I looked at each other and just shook our heads.

"Your dad thinks he is slick," I said laughing.

"Oh you ain't seen nothing yet" she replied.

We began talking she asked me questions about my job, my life and just basic things. I was so surprised by the manner in which she conversed with me. She was very well spoken and I can tell that she and Jayson were extremely close. We just laughed and talked. I asked her about basketball and if she wanted to go to college. I was taken back when she told me that she wanted to be a doctor. Pediatrics to be exact and I praised her for that. I could not help by to admire the way Jayson and her mother had raised her. I could not forget to tell him that later.

"Let's go see what's taking your dad so long with this food" I said.

We both walked in the kitchen and Jayson was preparing the table we joined and helped.

He made both of our plates and we all sat to eat.

"Do you guys mind if we say grace?" I asked.

"That would be nice" Mariah smiled.

We held hands and I blessed our food. We ate, talked, and laughed. I couldn't believe just how well the evening was going before I knew it was 10:45pm.

"Well it was very nice to meet you again Lauren, but dad I'm gonna go home tonight because I forgot to grab my book bag but I'll stay with you this weekend. Ok?" she said.

"That's cool just make sure you go straight home and call me soon as you get there. It shouldn't take you that long." He said and gave her a hug and a kiss.

"I'll be right back I'm going to walk her to the car." He said looking at me.

"Of course, Bye Mariah it was very nice meeting you and oh and girl check out Gucci they have some super cute new things" I said.

"Yes. I will thank you," she said.

Jayson:

Damn I don't know if God is looking out for ya boy or what cause that shit couldn't have went any smoother.

"I see why you like her dad," Mariah said breaking my thoughts.

"Shes's cool right?" I asked.

'Yes and she is very pretty I think we may have found a winner." She laughed.

'Well I'm glad you like her because I do too for real Raih" I said.

"I can tell dad. The way you look at her when she talks is cute. You wanted my approval and you got it. Now don't hurt her and get back in the house old man" she said hugging me.

"Thanks babygirl, drive safe and call me soon as you get there" I sais shutting her car door.

"Love you daddy"

"I love you too baby"

Mariah pulled off and I watched her leave until her car disappeared so I headed back into the house. Lauren was in the kitchen cleaning up.

"No. you don't have to do that" I said taking the plate out her hand.

She just smiled.

"I don't mind at all" she said.

"So did you enjoy your dinner?" I asked. I was wondering how she was feeling.

"It was very good I must admit you are a good cook Mr. Black and your daughter is wonderful. She is so sweet and I can't believe that she remembered me. That's so crazy how small the world is. Who would have known? You did a great job raising her and I admire ya'll relationship" she said.

"Yeah, that's crazy I was looking like WTF" I laughed.

"Although I was totally blindsided, you did not remind me that she would be joining us today and I'm in here looking like work" she said laughing but I can tell she was serious.

"I told you that you looked good already didn't I?" I said grabbing her from behind.

I wrapped my arms around her and kissed her neck. Then I turned her around to face me and kissed her lips. They were so soft.

"I had a good time tonight like always, can I ask you a favor" I asked.

"Shoot"

"Can you stay the night with me? I don't except anything I just want to sleep with you and hold you. I mean you are going out of town for a week. I'm gonna miss you!" I said.

Just as she was answering the phone rang it was Mariah letting me know she was home.

"Well" I said.

"How can I turn that invitation down?" she smiled.

Damn her smile was intoxicating. This girl had me wide the fuck open.

"Well is there a Walmart around here because I need a bonnet I cannot mess up this blowout" she was cracking up.

"Your boujee ass don't carry a bonnet in your purse?" I joked.

"No I do not. I haven't been having any night caps lately" she smiled.

"Let me see, I think Mariah has brand new ones upstairs because she loses them often." I said.

I returned back downstairs with a fresh in the pack bonnet. "Today is just your lucky day shorty"

We laughed.

"I have some new basketball shorts and T-shirt I'm sure you want to bathe. I will run you some water in the bathroom in my room and you can do your thing. I want you to be comfortable." I said.

"Yes. I need to get out of these clothes" she said.

"I'll just be in my office making a few calls until you finish and then we can watch a movie or something"

"Sounds good, hopefully I don't fall asleep on you. I'm a grandma" she laughed.

"That's okay to as long as you're here. Oh and I don't know about a grandma remember I seen you turning up in the club" I joked.

"Whatever" she laughed.

I headed to my office giving her some space. I trusted her in my home something told me she wouldn't go snooping in my stuff like normal nosey bitches always looking for something until they find it and then they want to be hurt and in they feelings.

I had put my phone on silent I didn't want any interruptions tonight. I did see that KP called and I also had 13 missed calls from Nyah. I hadn't been talking to her since I met Lauren and she wasn't to fond of me just cutting her off. But Nyah was nothing at all like the woman I would be with she was more so some convenient pussy. I looked out for her and she was cool. That was it she wasn't my girl but you couldn't tell her that.

I figured that it wasn't too important or KP would've hit me right back but I hit him back anyways.

"Whats good bro?" I said into the phone.

"Shit, fam was letting you know we was gonna have a little poker game but you aint answer." He said.

"I told you last time I'm not about to be fucking up my money fucking with you niggas" I laughed.

"Scary ass nigga" he said,

"Yeah ok, you don't believe that, but Mariah came over and met Lauren and shit" I said.

"word, how that go?" He asked.

"man bro they hit it off immediately"

"that's whats up fam, Mariah don't like nobody so you know shorty legit" KP said.

"that's exactly what I was thinking" I said.

"Get with me tomorrow bro my little shorty beeping in"

"Aight"

Tomorrow I planned on really breaking it off with Nyah cause I don't want no fucking problems. I went over a few reports from the club, signed a few checks for the laundromat. I could hear Lauren coming down the hallway she walked in the office sexy as fuck. My dick instantly got hard. She pulled her hair up in a ponytail and she looks so beautiful in the shorts and t-shirt. She came around my desk and sat on my lap.

"You smell good baby" I kissed her. She just looked at me directly in my eyes.

I told myself I would be a gentleman but fuck that I been dying to taste that pussy and I can't fight it no more. I stood up and began taking off her clothes. Lifting her shirt over her head and kissing her stomach and began caressing her I removed the shorts and exposed her beautiful naked body. He skin was soft as butter. Damn she was a work of art. Everything was in tack and her ass was stupid big. I spun her around her ass was directly on my dick. I used one hand to grabbed both her hands putting them above her head. I took my other sliding it down her body to arch her lower back just right then I spread her legs apart, as I began spreading them I could feel her getting wetter and soaking my fingers so I started to massage her clit and sucking on her neck at the same time. She let out a small moan and I slid right in from the back. She gasped and began to buckle but I gripped her waist tight and put her right back in the perfect position. I started stroking her slow and long, then fast and then slow again. She started convulsing with pleasure. After the first nut I turned her over we were face to face. I placed her on my desk right on the edge. I got on my knees and lifted her legs over my shoulders. I sucked and licked her pussy slow and sloppy. She arched her back in pleasure and grabbed my head. I started sucking her clit and I could tell I had hit the spot by the way her body was responding. She moaned my name so loud and telling me not to stop. I had no intentions and stopping. Her pussy was like water and tasted so good.

"Cum in my mouth: I said still licking and sucking.

She was just about to explode, her legs shook uncontrollably so I sped up my pace I wasn't stopping or backing down

"Oh my God, Oh my God" she moaned digging her nails deep in my back.

I swallowed every bit of her juices then stood up and picked her up walking her to my bedroom. I placed her on the bed. She was blushing and smiling. Damn she was so fucking sexy.

She grabbed me down and began kissing me passionately. She pushed me down on the bed and slide down on my dick, I felt every inch of her walls so tight and warm.

She rode me with precision as if she was riding a horse. Up, down and back up. She never once lost rhythm and she didn't use any hands. She rode dick like a fucking pro.

"damn baby" I said

Lauren spun around and began riding me backwards. I gripped her ass as it bounced up and down. I slowed her paced gripping her hips. She was riding me so good I didn't want to bust. But she wasn't stopping.

She rode faster, faster, moaned louder, and louder.

"Cum with me" she said.

I couldn't take it anymore.

"I'm cumming Jayson I'm cumming," she moaned.

"Damn me too"

We came together and she collapsed on top of me. I held her tight and we drifted off to sleep.

Lauren:

When I woke up Jayson was not in the bed and I had clearly over slept it was 8:30am. WTF. I needed to get home and get ready for work. I cannot believe that he let me sleep. I cannot believe that I fucked him last night. I was doing so good holding out. But damn it was so worth it. That man is talented with his tongue for sure and I was not excepting the dick to be that good.

I was instantly turned on when I seen the dick print in his sweat pants yesterday.

My phone was downstairs in my bag. So I got up and put on his robe hanging on the door and went to at least call and let them know I'd be running late. Just as I was heading down stairs, Jayson came from behind startling me slightly.

"Good Morning Beautiful" He said.

"Good Morning to you too" I smiled.

"Why did you let me over sleep you know I have to get to work now I'm late" I laughed.

"I apologize you were sleeping so peacefully and I didn't want to wake you, Plus I figured you were tired after that performance last night. By the way who was that Lauren 2.0?" he laughed.

"Oh my god, shut up" I smacked his arm.

I was so embarrassed. I just had an instant flash back and instant got wet.

"Do you have extra toothbrushes?" I asked.

"Yes in the medicine cabinet" he replied.

I went to brush my teeth and make sure I wasn't looking too bad. I went in the bathroom and damn I was glowing and blushing. I just could not stop picturing the way he looked eating my pussy. If I wasn't falling in love than I don't know what to call it. As the saying goes if I'm wrong then I don't want to be right.

Jayson knocked on the door asking to grab something.

"Do you always walk around with your shirt off" I asked admiring all his tattoos, which I loved by the way. It was something about a fine ass nigga with tattoos.

He laughed.

He just stood there staring at me while I brushed my teeth.

"What?" I asked.

"You are just very beautiful even when you wake up in the morning. I wouldn't mind waking up to you daily." He said.

This man knew exactly what to say at all the right moments. He was such a sweetheart.

"I mean that doesn't sound too bad. Maybe I'll spend the night more often" I smiled.

"I'll take that for now, but would you be offended if I asked you to skip work today?" he asked.

"Offended no. However, I have to decline I just have to get some work done before I leave in a few days. Plus that would not be very professional seeing I am already late" I laughed.

"I understand. Can I take you to dinner later?" he said.

"I actually have to pack but how about you come over my

place later and maybe we can order in or I can whip

something up" I said.

"Cool"

"Now get out so I can shower please"

"You sure you don't need help?" he asked.

"As tempting as that sounds. I don't want to start

anything I don't have time to finish" I replied

"You right" he just laughed and walked out the bathroom.

After showering and throwing on my clothes I headed to

the office. Thank God I had a few extra outfits there

because I just did not have time to go all the way home.

I headed into my office and Justice had a few notes

waiting for me and I had missed a few calls and some

emails. I was feeling refreshed and ready to work. It had

been a long while since I had sex and damn that was much needed to release that pinned up frustration.

I had a 12 o'clock meeting with my client to prepare his statement. Although we were taking a risk by having him testify, it was one that I was willing to take and could definitely work in our favor but he had to be well prepared for cross-examination.

"Lauren. Mr. Wells is here" Justice buzzed the intercom.

"Send him back," I said.

Rashaad Wells was my 22 year old client facing murder charges. He always came into my office looking like a dope boy and I would always remind him that he needed to tighten up his image. He was good at taking my advice and normally listened to what I told him.

"What's up Ms. Young" he said sitting down.

"Hello Rashaad, how is everything going?" I said.

"Just been laying low and staying out the way like you asked" he replied.

"Good. We are coming up on trial in two weeks and you don't need to do anything to make yourself look bad or get your bail revoked," I said.

"Right that's why I been chillin" said Rashaad.

"Let's go over your testimony and then I'll cross examine you. Everything has to be on point Rashaad. You have to control your emotions and your facial expressions the jury will be paying attention to all of that, you understand?" I asked.

After a few hours of preparing perfecting the testimony, I was confident that Rashaad would be able to handle getting on that stand and I was sure that things would go in our favor. Now that I had a grasp on this case and feeling even more confident, I could now get ready to go see my family.

CHAPTER 5

The next few days flew by Jayson had dropped me off at the airport and I was headed back to North Carolina for the first time in years. When I stepped off the plane it was such a bittersweet feeling being home stirred up many emotions that I was able to keep bottled up inside being in Erie.

Of course, London and Mommy were right there waiting for me.

I ran and hugged my mom so tight. I had missed her dearly.

"Hey mommy. You look so good" I kissed her and hugged her tighter.

"You too baby, I see you been eating good girl, you getting thick" she joked.

"La-la Lauren" London chimed.

"Pooh" I kissed and hugged my sister.

I could not wait to just kick it with them and relax.

We headed back to the house and pulled in the driveway

once again, this feeling came over me being back in my

family home after all these years.

"I know you only been here for a hot second but you

gotta fill us in on your new boo" London said.

"Yes you do" Mommy cosigned.

We sat down, mommy poured some wine, and it felt so

good to be talking to them. I filled them in on everything

and of course, my mom and sister wanted to know if the

dick was good. I know it sounds crazy but that's how

we've always been mommy was our best friend and we

talked about everything no matter how bad or crazy it

was. So I didn't spare any detail when telling them about

me and Jayson's sexual encounter the other night.

My mom was proud that I was able to hold out as long as

I did and so was I honestly. I told them that I thought he

was the one and just how much of a bond we had. I can tell that they were happy for me. My mom knew that I had been through a lot. And just how much of a void it left in my heart losing my dad so she was overjoyed to know that someone was loving me properly. For the first time in a long time, I was truly happy and it had a lot to do with Mr. Black.

Jayson:

I was missing my lady but I needed a little more time to figure out this shit with Juan and I'm gonna have a talk with Taylor too and pay Nyah a visit so she knew that it was a wrap. On my way uptown I couldn't help but notice the young nigga Chris on the block. I admired the youngin he was a true hustler. Kinda reminded me of myself growing up so I got out and hollered at him for a minute. I don't really be out on the blocks no more but sometimes it was a humbling reminder of the days on my way to the top.

"What up O.G" Chris said.

I gave him dap and we chopped it up for a few.

"I see you young nigga" I said walked away after our few minute conversation.

I had just got back in my car and all the sudden I hear shots,

POW, POW, POW, POW, POW. I ducked by at the same time grabbing the strap out the glow box.

I see Chris bussin back but the car had sped off. I didn't get a good look at shit.

I ran over and the young nigga was clearly hit. Someone had already called 911 cause I could hear the sirens already.

Blood was leaking from his chest. He was hit badly.

"Hold on young nigga, keep breathing" I said. I took my jacket and applied some pressure. I couldn't let the little nigga die not on my watch.

The ambulance came just in time and I got in my ride and met them at the hospital. When I got there, the hospital was on lock. His family was up there deep. I hit KP but he was already on his way so I just waited for him before I left.

KP pulled up and I got in his car.

"Word on the street the young nigga must've got into with some other little nigga's over some bread and they came bussin" KP said.

"Fuck, this just gonna slow up money over that way" I said.

"Word and now ain't they time" KP replied.

"Right you know I don't handle the street that your area G, but we gotta see exactly what's up and make sure this shit don't start a fucking battle" I said seriously.

"I already got the young niggas on ice by the time we get back in a few days shit should be calm" KP said.

"Cool. Keep me posted on Chris I gotta get out this bloody shit" I got out and headed to my ride.

Only to get stop my Dickhead 1 and Dickhead 2 asking me to come to the station and make a statement.

"Ya'll know damn well I ain't making no statement. Now get the fuck out my face," I laughed and kept fucking walking.

Detective James and Knowles been on my ass since I was a young boy all they did was fuck with me growing up it pissed them off that they could never tie me to anything. What the fuck was they doing down here any ways they are narcotics.

Something in my gut told me that things was about to get crazy. Fuck. I don't have time for this shit not right now. I headed to shower and change than over by Nyah spot. She lived out west in a nice quiet neighborhood. Nyah wasn't a bad girl at all she was pretty she just wasn't wife material she wanted to party and be seen. She had a job and worked but she needed my help more and more lately.

I pulled up and she was sitting on the porch running her fucking mouth like always. When she seen me she hung up and instantly started making a scene. This was the shit I was talking about with her just too loud and ghetto.

"Man get the fuck in the house and be quiet" I grabbed her arm lightly.

"I know you seen me calling don't think I ain't here you been running around with some little lawyer bitch" Nyah was yelling.

"Lower your fucking voice and this my last time telling you that" I said sternly.

She knew I was serious in my tone.

"I just don't get why you been giving me the cold shoulder." She said much more quietly.

"I do not want to lead you on or play with your feelings. I'm in a relationship now Nyah and we gotta cut ties." I said.

She looked shocked as fuck I mean I'd been fucking Nyah for years now shit I was fucking around with her while I was with Taylor.

"You know what I'm not begging no nigga to stay anywhere I hope the bitch makes you happy" she said real sarcastic.

"Tomorrow I'll wire 10,000 in your account that should cover your bills for a while" I said and left out.

I wasn't a dirty ass nigga I know Nyah had depended on me helping her out with her bills yeah shorty worked and shit but I had made her comfortable and exposed her to an expensive lifestyle but that wasn't my problem anymore. My main focus was Lauren I was not playing around with these bitches that I could never even see myself with.

I was hoping that Nyah would just respect it and move on but something told me that she would make some noise soon.

But until then I would consider her handled cause she was the least of my worries I had way more important shit that needed my immediate attention. This situation with Chris was on my brain heavy this is the exact reason why I decided to become a businessman. The streets only lead to death or jail and lucky I had avoided both. I had no intentions on experiencing them either. I knew that KP could handle them young niggas but I had a feeling that things would get ugly and I needed as much information as I could get so I would remain ahead of the game. Even though I was the furthest from the streets one wrong move could put all my business in jeopardy.

I made a call out west to my people and put them deep and now it was a waiting game because one thing for certain and two things for sure the streets always talked.

I felt my phone buzz it was Lauren.

Damn I had been so caught up I had not called to see how her flight was.

"Hello beautiful" I answered.

"Well hey Mr. Black" she responded.

"Why so formal miss lady," I asked.

"Just checking up on you hoping you haven't found any trouble since I've been gone" she laughed.

"Not at all" I lied.

I just didn't want to scare her and upset her trip so I would just fill her in when she returned.

"Well it feels really good to be home and I can't wait to come back hopefully you can join me next time. My family has been grilling me about you the moment I stepped off the plane. Geesh." She said.

"I look forward to it, I want you to enjoy yourself. I have a few things to handle and then I will call you a little later" I said.

"Ok babe. Talk to you later" she said.

CHAPTER 6

Lauren:

I could tell in Jayson's voice that something was off but I did not want to press the issue. I am sure if it is important he will tell me. I needed to be getting dressed anyways my brother were taking me out tonight and I was ready to let loose.

I was back home and the streets of Charlotte had not seen me since I was a young girl. Funny thing is the last name Young held so much weight. My dad once ran this entire side of the map and that rep of being his daughter just never died. Although I wear my name proudly, it is a bit of a gift and a curse but I am finally glad to have come into my own and just be Lauren.

There was a light tap on the door.

"Come in" I said.

Kyree walked in with the biggest smile on his face. I truly loved my brother so much he was just everything to me.

"Wassup baby why you smiling" I said smiling.

"Shit just happy to see you sis" he laid across my bed.

"I know it feels good to be home," I said.

"Yeah I miss having you around but I am super proud of you" he said.

"Thank you so much don't make me cry" I said tearing up.

"Damn, you still a cry baby" he laughed.

I just bussed out laughing.

"Yes, yes I am," we laughed together.

"Get dressed kid we gonna do dinner first and then we will head down to The Palace" he said.

"Sounds good because I'm starving." I said.

Kyree headed out the door and he was reading a text and yelled "FUCK"

"You good bro" I asked

"Yeah sis I'm cool I'll see you in a minute" he said.

I knew my brother was lying and I wished my brothers would just leave the streets alone. I know they had enough money and businesses but it was like an addiction or something. They wanted to be just like our dad and honestly, I believe it was the stress from the streets that killed him. I would just hate for anything to happen to one of them it is just not worth it to me.

Kyree:

How the fuck did these dumb asses fuck that shit up. Damn I guess somethings you got to handle yourself if you want them done right. Guess I'll have to take a trip up North.

Lauren:

Being out with my siblings tonight felt so good. We turned all the way the fuck up our section was so fuckin LIT. We popped bottle after bottle and Jamie just kept them coming. They loved my brothers and it showed. London and I danced all night cause the DJ was cutting up we couldn't sit down if we wanted. It was almost 4am and about time for the club to close. Some chicks were

eyeballing London for the last 45 minutes. I nudged my

sister.

"You see this? " I looked their way and asked.

"Oh yeah you know I'm on" she responded.

"Do we gotta check these hoes?" I asked.

Don't let the lawyer shit fool you because if I had to get

my hands dirty I would especially when it comes to my

siblings. Therefore, my awareness at this point was

through the roof but the one girl headed toward us and

was briefly making small talk with my brother Jamie.

Maybe they were kicking it and she didn't know who I

was but still I got a bad vibe from the bitch and one thing

about me my instincts were almost always correct. I will

be cool for now but I never forget a face. London gave a

look and I knew my sister well enough that we were both

thinking the very same thing. Valet had pulled up the car

by the time we headed outside we got in the car and pulled off once again I noticed the two chicks from inside the club looking at my brother car. So I asked Jamie what was up and he just said it was cool that was business. I took his word and left it alone. We decided to go eat but remembered that there were leftovers at mommy's house. We all would much rather eat that then anything we could get this late.

The light was on in the living room when we got back to the house. Mommy was up watching TV.

"What you still doing up ma" we all asked.

"I didn't know I had a bed time" she laughed.

"It's late you okay" Jamie said.

"Yes. You guys I am fine I got up to get something to drink and noticed you all were still gone so I just came and watched some TV' she said.

We all raided the fridge I made my brothers plates and they left out. London said she was gonna stay in the guest bedroom and she headed to bed.

I was glad to get my mommy alone.

"Well I'm gonna ahead to bed" said mommy.

I followed her in her room and laid on her. She stroked my hair. It was as if I was 17 all over again.

"You sure you okay mom" I asked looking her in her eyes.

"Yes baby, just get lonely sometimes in this house so I be up often at night" she said.

"Awe mom you know I always told you that you can come visit me for a while" I said.

"I know baby." she said.

"You miss him huh?" I asked.

"Every single day" she replied.

It just broke my heart to know that my mom lived home alone. We had all grown up and moved on and she was by herself.

"You know me and your dad planned on traveling once you went away to school and we finally would have the house to ourselves," she said softly.

"I miss him so much too mommy" I said.

"I often think about moving because every single thing reminds me of him here but he was so happy to build this house for me I just can't seem to let it go" she said.

"You just need a small break from here come back with me when I go home. You can sit in on the trial and just spend a few weeks and see my new house" I said.

"You know what I think I may just do that baby girl" she smiled.

"I love you." I said.

"I love you more than anything" she kissed my head.

Before I knew it, I had drifted off to sleep. I woke up in my mom's bed and of course to the smell of breakfast.

I got up, went to the bathroom, brushed my teeth, and washed my face. When I got to the kitchen mommy was fixing me a plate.

"I heard you getting up, Good Morning Sunshine" she smiled.

"Good Morning Ma" I kisses her cheek..

"Hope you hungry I know you don't get to eat breakfast at home much your always at work so early." She said.

"Nothing like your breakfast anyways" I replied.

"Well you sister headed out so it's just us" she said.

"I'm glad we got to talk last night mommy, you know sometimes I just miss being home" I said.

"I know you do but you're living your dreams pumpkin" she said.

My mom always knew exactly what to say.

"Well we have the party tonight so we need to get with the planner and make sure everything goes off without a hitch." she said.

"Sounds good it should be a great night" I said.

"Yes I'm gonna turn up" she laughed.

"Ma, what you know about turning up" I laughed.

"Don't let this age fool you, ya momma still got it. Where you think you got it from" She teased.

We both cracked up but I knew she was serious.

"Girl wait till you see my dress" she said.

"Oh ok ma you gonna kill it?" I asked.

"You already know," she said walking away.

I was happy she was happy to be honest she hasn't really been herself since I got here but I'm sure my siblings are way too caught up to even notice what the hell I would be talking about. Its things like this that make me wonder if being so far from her for all these years was a good idea.

I was so caught up in my own personal battles that I

kinda forgot about what she was going through.

However, I was going to change all of that.

When we arrived at the venue, I was in awe. My mom

outdid herself with this party this shit looked like a

wedding. Every single fucking detail was perfect. This

was a Jackie Young party cause my mom believed in "do

it right or don't do it at all" and she lived up to it in

everything she did.

"They did a good job huh?" she asked.

"Yes. They did," I said still looking around.

"I need you to make sure your brother is on time" she

said.

"I will try my best" I said.

Jayson:

"Always a pleasure" I said shaking Juan's hand.

"Likewise" he responded.

Just like that, I had finally made the connection between Juan and KP. I was OUT. I had more than enough money and my businesses were thriving. It was a good day and I planned to make it an even better night.

"So you finally out?" KP said.

"Yeah man," I said feeling good.

"We came along way who ever thought we would see this much money," he said.

"I always knew we would be successful K. We had hearts of lions," I said.

I had not told anyone what I was planning to do but I was trusting my heart and I just knew I was making the right decision.

"I got to run bro, got a flight to catch" I said.

"Where you headed now fam," he asked.

"North Carolina" I smiled.

"Go get your bitch, my nigga" he laughed.

That is exactly what I planned on doing. I was glad this meeting went so smooth and I could surprise Lauren I knew her family meant the world to her and she really was disappointed that I couldn't make the party so I know she is going to be happy.

When I landed in Charlotte, I caught a taxi to my hotel. Lauren had no clue when I asked her what was the name of the hotel the party was at that I was actually picking her for information.

I had been all over the world, surprisingly this was one place on my list I had yet to visit, and so far I was impressed at the amount of black people here getting to it.

I checked into the Ritz Carlton Downtown.

I texted Lauren and asked her to send me a picture when she was dressed.

I began to get myself together tonight was a special occasion so I had to really put my shit on tonight.

I had my tan Gucci suit tailored perfectly. My brown dress shirt complemented my socks, bow tie and shoes. I had to do a double take in the mirror a nigga was looking like money. Couple pumps of the Gucci Guilty cologne and it was show time.

CHAPTER 7

Lauren:

I had forgotten what it was like getting dressed in the house with my mom and my sister. We had the music blasting my mom was playing Luther Vandross and we were jamming. Funny thing is we had 4 bathrooms but we were in mommy's bathroom helping each other get flawless.

My mom looked ravishing in her rose gold dress. London was beautiful in her all white. And of course, my red dress was beyond perfect. We were making perfect time tonight was not a night to be fashionable late. So we all headed out the door to make it downtown.

I called Jamie on the way and surprisingly he was leaving his house he said. I just knew tonight would be perfect. Only thing missing was daddy but I didn't want to be sad tonight I wanted to enjoy each and every moment with my family because I'd be back home in two days.

When we pulled up the cars were everywhere. My brother was a good nigga and he had brought the city out tonight.

Jamie stepped in the building looking so fine and his girl Ciara looked just as gorgeous on his arm. My brother had on Gucci from head to toe he wasn't your suit wearing

kinda person but his linen was definitely grown man

tonight.

Kyree was not far behind with his LV everything. I must

say my whole family did not come to play tonight.

"Where is your date bro?" I asked Kyree

"Now why would I bring sand to the beach?" he laughed.

Mommy just shook her head and London agreed.

The night was getting started and everyone was enjoying

themselves. The drinks were flowing, the food was good

and my family was happy. My mom and grandma MiMi

were the life of the party they fast danced all night and of

course, I had to join in. We danced and laughed and

danced some more. The photographer came around and

we all took a gorgeous photo I could not forget to get a

copy before I left. That was most certainly going up in

my house.

We was just about to sing Happy Birthday when I heard someone come behind me and say, "Excuse me Miss Lady"

I turned around and I could not believe my eyes. Jayson was standing there with a glass of champagne in his hand smiling from ear to ear looking so fucking fine.

"What, what are you doing here?" I asked.

"I couldn't let my lady be alone tonight?" he said giving me a long hug and kiss.

"I don't know what to say, you just never cease to amaze me. I thought you had business," I said.

"I did and I finished early so I caught a flight. You know boss shit," he laughed.

"Well I am so glad that the boss came" I blushed.

"You look so stunning" he whispered in my ear.

"You don't look to bad yourself," I whispered back.

"I hope I get to take that dress off later," he said.

"Well I was thinking maybe we leave it on" I winked.

He sipped his drink and smiled. I could tell he was getting hard and honestly, I was ready to leave with him at that point. I was so caught up in our eye contact that I never even noticed my brother Kyree and London heading my way until I heard.

"Excuse Me," said London.

I knew they must've been watching the whole thing.

"So is this who I think it is?" said London.

"Yes. To my surprise this is um Jayson" I began to say.

"Hello I'm Jayson your sister's boyfriend," he said.

I was so nervous like a little girl. Kyree had a look as if he was feeling him out and London looked as if she had a seen a meal.

"Nice to finally meet you" London said.

"Yes. I have heard so much about you all its my pleasure" Jayson said.

Before I could even introduce them, Kyree had asked Jayson if they could talk and out of nowhere I seen Jamie heading over. I was mortified I did not want them to embarrass me in any way. I was about to step in but Jayson motioned for me to stay behind.

After what seemed to be an hour, they all returned laughing and smiling. I was so relieved my brother's opinion mattered more than anything and I just wanted them to like him as much as I did.

Kyree whispered in my ear "you got my approval little sis he a good nigga I can tell."

That was all I needed to hear Kyree was so much like me he was a great judge of character and if he said it was cool then I was confident everything I had been feeling was right.

I walked Jayson over to meet my mom and grandma.

"Mommy I'd like you to meet Jayson" I said.

"Oh my well hello handsome it is nice to meet the mystery man I been hearing about" she said.

"Nice to meet you Mrs. Young I see exactly where Lauren gets her beauty" he said giving her a hug.

"And smells good" she said smiling.

"Mommmm" I said.

"Thank You" he said.

I just shook my head and laughed. They were not embarrassing me too much so I just went along with it.

"Can I have this dance" Jayson asked mommy.

I was super shocked I didn't even know he danced.

"Oh Lauren you better watch him, I may steal him" mommy said taking his hand.

And they disappeared to the dance floor I could see they were talking and having a good time. I was in amazement he was winning my family over by the minute which was not an easy task. More and more I began to think this man was an angel in disguise.

Finally he headed back to where I was standing.

"I'm sorry," he said.

"Sorry for what" I asked.

"I haven't spent any time with you all night" he said.

"It's okay. I'm glad you are getting to know my family" I said.

"Me too you have something special. Something I never had growing up its dope and your mom she is all that. Man I didn't think she could dance like that" he smiled.

"Yes. She is a hot mess" I laughed.

"You want something else to drink?" he asked.

"Sure I could go for one more I think you tryna get me drunk" I responded.

"Maybe, I'll be right back and I promise you will have me all to yourself" he winked.

Suddenly the lights got dim but for some reason not around me as if there was a spotlight directly where I was standing.

Jayson headed back my way and the server was behind him with a tray with a few bottles of champagne.

This man had to get the whole bottle I thought to myself.

I was most certainly gonna perform in the bed tonight.

As he got closer to me the look on his face was all weird.

"What's wrong" I asked.

But before he even answered my question he began to drop down on one knee.

"OMG. What are you doing" I whispered.

At this point all eyes were on us. And I could not believe what was happening.

He grabbed my hand and in his other hand was a big red box.

"Lauren from the very first day that I laid my eyes on you I knew that you were something special and the moment that you allowed me in your world I told myself I would never let you go. You are perfect, your smart, beautiful, funny and caring. You have something that speaks to the man inside of me. I had been asking God to send me a wife but instead he sent me an angel and I am standing her in front of your entire family hoping that you will continue to make me the luckiest man on Earth and be my wife. Lauren Young will you marry me?" he asked. I could not stop the tears from falling I was so shocked and overwhelmed. This was all so sudden and I never really knew that he felt this strong. Normally I think everything out but this time I was trusting my heart.

"Yes. Yes baby I will marry you" I said.

Jayson opened the box and revealed the most beautiful 5 carats VVS diamond ring damn near blinding me. I could not take my eyes off it as he placed it on my finger. The center stone was so huge and there were two smaller stones on each side. I had never seen anything so beautiful in my life.

I kissed him passionately and I could not let him go. I was crying, smiling, and just so overjoyed. Everything in my life seemed to be aligning up. Just as I had really given up on love but this man came and changed all of that and he did it in such a perfect way. All my family came rushing over to see the ring.

"BITCHHHHHHHHH YESSSSS" said London.

"I am so happy for you baby" mommy hugged me with tears in her eyes.

Welcome to the family" she said to Jayson.

"Thank you, I won't disappoint you Mrs. Jackie," he said to her.

My brother both hugged me and kissed me telling me how happy they were for me. Jayson, Jamie and Kyree dapped each other up and by their look I can tell they had a mutual respect for one another. That was a blessing. I just still could not believe this was happening.

This night had become a celebration for sure. The DJ turned the music back up and we all headed to the floor. He got on the mic and congratulated Jayson and myself and dedicated Wale Matrimony to us. I could not stop showing off my ring as we danced.

After a about another hour of partying with my family Jayson and I dipped off to his room.

We got on the elevator and just looked in each other's eyes for a brief moment. We shared the same brief stare the night in the club when we first met.

He pulled me close and kissed me on my neck.

"I love you" he whispered in my ear.

"I love you too" I responded.

We could barely make it to his room by the time we reached the door my dress was halfway unzipped and I had his shirt fully unbuttoned. I was ready to make love to my fiancé like never before. Once inside he sat me on the bed, removed my shoes and dress and began kissing and massaging my feet. He kissed every inch of my body starting at my toes but stopping at my inner thighs. He licked and nibbling and kissed teasing my body making me cum in anticipation. I was patient and enjoyed every moment watching him treat my entire body with so much love and affection. We shared brief moments of eye contact and each time he would say "I love you Lauren." It was like I was dreaming but I never wanted to wake up if I was.

He rolled me over laying me on my stomach he started massaging my back and ass but his tongue instantly replaced his hands. Before I knew it, my ass was in the air and Jayson was head first in my pussy. He licked form my clit to my ass not giving one more attention then the other. I was in pure ecstasy and came not once but twice in the matter of minutes, each time I tried to run he grabbed me back and tasted more and more. I moaned his name softly and gripped the sheets before I was about to explode again he flipped me on my back and slip right into all my wetness. I grabbed his body tight and we made love. He took his time and rocked my body slowly with strong deep strokes. With each stroke, I dug my nails deeper into his back. Jayson kissed and sucked my neck as he continued to dick me down.

"Don't stop bae." I whispered.

He kissed and sucked my lips telling me he wasn't stopping.

"This my pussy forever" he asked.

"Yes it is" I moaned.

"You love me" he asked.

"I love you so much" I moaned.

He felt so good. It was as if our bodies had became one the rhythm was slow and smooth but so passionate. We continued to please each other until the wee hours of the morning. I realized that I had not even told my family I was leaving but I am sure they got the picture. I just wanted to enjoy the moment and enjoy my future.

"Can I ask you a question?" I asked.

"Shoot" he said.

"Have you ever dreamed about something that you never knew even existed?" I asked.

"Yes. I have and it's looking me in face right now." He responded.

I was truly in love, he had managed to break every wall down, and my heart was in his hands. It never once crossed my mind that he would ever hurt me. We talked until the sun came up and neither one of us seemed to be tired I don't ever remember falling asleep but when I did open my eyes. I was lying on his chest and he was sleeping so peacefully, so comfortable. I paid attention to his breathing and listened to his heartbeat there was something so calm about him. It seemed as though there were no other people in the world but us.

I just laid there thinking and soon I drifted back off to sleep.

Jayson:

She was sleeping so peaceful that I didn't want to wake her up. Her natural beauty was breathtaking and I was more than prepared to make her my wife. I knew that she was surprised last night and shit, I still can't believe it myself. I had not even told my niggas nor did I tell my baby girl but I knew they both would be happy for me.

Last night was a good night and it turned out perfect.

Lauren didn't have a clue that when I asked her mother to

dance I asked if I could marry her daughter. She had her

reservations but she agreed. As for her brothers they

were bosses like me and we had a mutual respect. Of

course they wanted to make sure I didn't hurt their baby

sister and I had to respect that any real man would. But of

course, the street in me made me want to do my

homework on them. I needed to know exactly what I was

getting myself into and they seemed to be getting some

real paper I had noticed the love they got last night.

"Good Morning sleeping beauty" I said.

I heard her creep up behind me.

"Good Morning Baby" she said wrapping her arms

around me.

"We should probably head over to my mom's I am sure they are wondering why we didn't return back to the party last night" she said.

"That's cool you wanna join me for a shower" I said.

"Well I'm not sure. We may not make it anywhere" she laughed.

"That's cool too as long as I'm here with you" I smiled.

We showered and got dressed and headed to her mom's house once we arrived I was impressed. We had pulled up at the same time as her brother Jamie.

"I see ya'll still alive" he joked dapping me up and giving Lauren a hug.

"Yes" she blushed.

I could see his girl admiring Lauren's ring but not really saying much it was obvious she was ready to be more than just a girlfriend.

"I am happy for you guys though look like we will be having a wedding." said Jamie

"Thanks" I said.

We all headed inside, Mrs. Young was cooking, and I had not smelled food that good since my grandma had passed away.

I admired from a far just how well their family interacted with each other. It made me wonder if I would have ever chosen to be in the street if I had the love and support of a family. This was all the reason I was ready to be a family man. We would be heading back to Erie tomorrow so I wanted Lauren to enjoy her family as much as she could. I could tell that she was missed just being around them by the way she was smiling and glowing. She was truly a blessing.

"So Jayson Lauren tells us that you own a nightclub" Mrs. Young asked breaking my thoughts.

"Yes I do" I said.

"Do you like that business my husband owned a club also" she said. "It was overwhelming at times."

"I do enjoy it but you are right at times it can be a bit much but my town is much smaller then here so I can only image" I responded.

"Yeah that shit used to be a lot and the woman oh my they were savages" she shook her head.

"You are right about that but I won't have any of those issues" I said. I could tell she was trying to feel me out and see if I was a cheater, I was amused. Mrs. Jackie was definitely up on game.

"Aye yo Jayson you ain't gotta sit over there and let them pick your brain all day" Kyree said motioning for me to come outback with them. I was low key relieved and I wanted to see what was up with her brothers a little more.

I headed out back and left Lauren to kick it with her mom and sister.

"Thanks" I laughed.

We made some small talk but then the conversation switched to business and I was getting the information I needed. Just like I thought, they were moving heavy weight all through the South I had to respect it. Had it been a few years earlier I would have wanted in. I could tell that Jamie was more the brains of everything and Kyree was the muscle. I also picked up that Kyree was more involved in the legal business. I am sure that's why he and Lauren are extremely close.

I invited them up to check out the club. So far, I had no ill feeling or thought we would have problems. They could recognize a real nigga and as long as the line of respect was never crossed, we would be cool.

"So you really ready to settle down" Jamie asked.

"Yeah man it's nothing out here" I said.

"I know but damn answering to the same woman forever" he laughed.

"You don't want to be married to your old lady" I said.

"Ciara she is wife material I'm just not ready and I don't even want to play with that marriage shit just to say I'm married" he said.

"I can feel that" I said.

"Yeah I haven't found the one yet. None of these bitches ain't like my mom or my sisters," Kyree added.

"Hell naw they ain't" Jamie said.

"You lucky though cause baby sis different she like one of a kind" Kyree said to me.

I could not even argue with that he was absolutely right. She was special and a rare breed. We continued to kick it but after a few hours, Lauren was ready to head back to the hotel. We had an early fight to catch back home and

KP texted and said it was important we link soon as I touch.

Lauren:

It was kind of bittersweet leaving my family but I was ready to get back home and I could not wait to show off this ring at the office. My mom would be coming up in a few weeks for a little while so I wasn't as sad because I knew I would see her soon.

I was exhausted so I slept most of the flight back home.

"Bae; I felt Jayson tapping me.

I opened my eyes in confusion.

"We about to land" he smiled.

"I'm sorry I was so tired" I said.

"It's cool I slept a little too and I know you need rest you about to have a big day tomorrow" he said.

The trial started at 7am tomorrow and I was getting nervous but ready.

"I know, I hope I do well" I said.

"You will baby don't even trip" he smiled kissing my hand.

"Thank You" I said.

We landed and got our luggage Jayson had a car waiting for us to get home.

"So I don't want to impose but what are we going to do about out living arraignments?" he asked.

"What do you mean?" I asked.

"I mean I want to wake up to you daily, you are going to be my wife soon" he said.

"Well for now until the wedding let's spend the nights together at my place or yours and then we can come up with a solution that is best for us both" I suggested.

"I can live with that for now" He said.

I guess I never even took a moment to realize that all of this was happening so fast. He had not even stayed the night at my house yet and I would be planning a wedding. All I could do was trust that God was leading me in the right direction.

After a good night's, rest it seemed that 6am rolled around so fast.

I got up, prayed, and put on my brand new navy blue and white pinstriped suit and my navy pumps.

I for damn sure looked the part. I met Rashaad in front of the Federal Court House and we walked in ready and prepared for the fight.

The prosecution had completed their opening statements and it was show time for me. I walked up to the jury and looked each one of them in the eyes.

"Members of the jury we are here today to prove that an innocent man is being charged with a crime that he did not commit. I trust that after review of all the facts and evidence both physical and testimonial that I will present during this trial that you will fulfill your civic duty, make the proper decision, and find my client not guilty. I am here to tell you that the prosecution will not meet there burden of proof, which is that my client did in fact commit criminal homicide BEYOND A REASONABLE DOUBT. Thank you" I said confidently.

Trial had officially begun and it was a back and forth battle between the prosecution and myself. They had presented the evidence and called up an eyewitness for testimony.

"Your honor, I object the last statement of Ms. Reed's testimony" I said.

"On what grounds Ms. Young," said the judge.

"Hearsay your honor" I replied.

"I object" the prosecution replied.

"Overruled, the last part of the testimony shall be removed due to its hearsay nature," the judge said.

We had finally presented the evidence and the judge

called a rest for the day we would began again tomorrow

at 7am.

Rashaad and I had a brief conversation and he was

looking pleased with the outcome of today as was

tomorrow and I would have the chance to get him on the

stand and his testimony could make or break this case. I

was feeling more confident than ever. I knew that my

performance today was stellar. It was as if I had been in

the courtroom all my life. I was confident and

comfortable. Once in the car I seen that Jayson had texted

and called me so returned his call, he had been crazy busy

since we got back from Charlotte and secretly I was cool

with it because it gave me time to just focus on work and

also really think if we were moving just a little too fast. I

didn't want to tell him my fear because I did not want

him to think I was reconsidering getting married. I mean

it wasn't like we would do the shit next week. We had plenty of time we could at least wait a year. I did need time to plan my wedding even though I had my wedding already planned since I was a little girl only thing missing all these years was my groom.

I headed home for the day I wanted to eat and just relax my mind for the next few days.

Tomorrow Morning 8am

"I would like to call my first witness to the stand" I stated.

"Can you please state your first and last name for the courts?" I asked.

"Rashaad Wells" he said.

"Mr. Wells can you please explain as specific as possible your whereabouts on the night on June 3rd, 2008?" I asked.

"I was leaving from the club and stopped by the Country Fair on Reed & 110th Street before heading back to my apartment." He stated just as we had rehearsed.

"Do you know about the time you left the club?" I asked.

"It was about 2:45am," he said.

"And can you tell me about the time you got home on the night in question?" I asked.

"It was about 3:40am" he responded.

"Is it correct that your house is about 10 minutes from the gas station that you stopped at?" I asked.

"Yes" he said.

"Are you aware that Ronald House was murdered at 3:00am" I asked.

"Yes" he said.

"Which means that during the time of his death you had to be in your car driving to your house?" I asked.

Just as I had planned the prosecution objected my question.

"On what grounds" said the judge.

"That is a leading question your honor," said the D.A.

I knew that it was a leading question and I wanted to see just how the D.A would respond.

"I will rephrase your honor" I stated.

"Overruled, Ms. Young please re- phrase" said the judge.

"Mr. Wells can you please explain you were you would have been at 3:00am" I asked.

"At 3:00 am I was driving in my car heading home after stopping and getting gas" Rashaad responded.

"Thank you Mr. Wells. Can you please for the courts tell me the make and model of your vehicle" I asked.

"I was driving a Silver Mercedes Benz Truck" he said.

"If I may direct everyone's attention to the video surveillance from the Country Fair. Furthermore I would like to take note of Mr. Wells car at the gas pump and please note the time stamp from the video" I said eyeing the jury.

"Mr. Wells is this your license plate number shown in this video # HB4434?" I asked.

"Yes" he responded.

Rashaad was doing a great job at just answering my question and not rambling off.

"As we can see this video has my client's car at the pump pulling off at approximately 2:52am" I said pointing to the screen.

"No further questions" said.

"Is the state prepared for cross examination" said the judge.

"May I approach" said the D.A

"Mr. Wells is it true that you and the deceased had prior violent history" said the D.A.

"The deceased and myself were not friends but we were not enemies" Rashaad answered.

"Is it true that the two of you had an intense conversation on the night in question at the club" said the D.A.

"No" said Rashaad.

"So the video of you and the deceased in the club is made up?" said the D.A.

"No, we did talk but it was not an intense conversation" said Rashaad.

"Might I ask what that conversation was pertaining to" asked the D.A.

"Business" said Rashaad.

"Business and is that short for drug dealings" said the D.A.

"Objection" I said.

"Mr. Levy please get to the question" said the judge.

"I apologize Your Honor, Mr. Wells what kind of business did you and the deceased have to discuss" he asked.

"We both own real estate and had mutual interest in a particular property" said Rashaad.

"Was that property lucrative enough for you to kill him?" said the D.A.

"Objection Your Honor, that is a leading question" I said.

"Sustained" said the Judge.

"No further questions" said the D.A.

His face was beet red and I could tell that the calmness of Rashaad was bothering him.

After the prosecution presented their final eyewitness testimony It was time for closing arguments and the jury would deliberate today.

"Ladies and gentlemen of the jury I would like to thank you for your time and dedication to these lengthy and overwhelming two days. We have come to the close and there is no more evidence that can be presented and no more testimony that will be heard. I want to ask you one final question. What have I proved to you? Have I convinced you beyond a reasonable doubt what occurred on the night in question. So much so that you don't have any doubts as to the issues that I have presented in the last two days? If you have any doubt about what the state had presented, then it is your civic duty to let my client go guilt cannot have any doubt. It is black and white. Ask yourself it is possible for Mr. Wells to commit the murder given the time seen on video. Is it possible to have left no physical evidence behind? With such little time there was so much room for error. When you go back to that room I just asked that you use only fact and no opinions. Make the right choice and send my client, an innocent man home. Thank You" I said.

The just went out and we were released for a break and time seemed to go so slow. The jury had not reached a verdict and the judge rested for the day we would pick back up tomorrow morning. I was so nervous I did not sleep all night. It was 2:16am I am sure he as sleeping but I just needed to vent.

The phone rang.

No answer.

Damn, he's probably sleeping but then my phone rang and it was him.

"Did I wake you" I said.

"What's wrong" Jayson said in a sleep voice.

"I can't sleep. I'm so nervous, what if I lose the case?" I was just rambling.

"Lauren calm down, You've worked hard and you gave it your all you were awesome in that court room just relax bae" he said.

It seemed that just hearing him say that my body began to calm down and I felt bad for waking him up.

"I am sorry for waking you" I said softly.

"Don't be your gonna be my wife soon and this is why after this case we need to talk about our living situation. I don't want to wake up without you anymore" he said.

"Yes we will, no go back to sleep see you tomorrow" I said.

"I love you" he said.

"I love you too" I replied.

I wasn't worried about the case anymore now I was worried about my future was I ready for all of this. I have waited my whole life to find a man like Jayson and now I am more scared than ever. I am not sure what I am scared of exactly. He loves and appreciates me. I guess I never really knew what that felt like because anything that I ever even considered to be love was nothing like this.

The past always hurt and nothing about the love that he brings hurts. It feels so good like too good. I was able to drift off to sleep with ease.

The morning came fast and we all gathered in back in the courtroom. The jury had reached a verdict.

"On the count of Murder in the first degree we find the defendant NOT GUILTY" said the jury spokesman.

"The count of manslaughter in the 3rd degree we find the defendant NOT GUILTY" she repeated.

They had found Rashaad not guilty on all charges.

"OMG" we did it I looked him in the eyes.

Rashaad gave me the biggest hug and said thank you.

I had never been more proud in my life. I had my first big case and I won!

Funny thing is I had a great feeling we would beat the case but now it was official. We walked out of that courtroom and the media was everywhere waiting to hear a statement. We gracefully declined. Rashaad wanted to get far away from that courtroom and I did not blame him. He thanked me once again.

"I'll be dropping off the retainer fee tomorrow I gotta keep you on the team Ms. Young." he said.

"Absolutely" I replied.

I couldn't hide the smile I had to call Jayson and tell him. He didn't answer.

Maybe he was busy I thought to myself. So I called my mom after but again no answer.

Damn where is everyone at I gotta share the good news.

I continue to walk to my car and was suddenly stopped by the honking of a horn clearly trying to get my attention.

"Excuse me" I heard the lady say.

I turned around and it was my mom and Jayson pulling up.

"I told you that I was coming up and what a better day than on your big day" she smiled getting out of the car.

"You guys have been pulling off a lot of surprises lately" I smiled.

"Congratulations" Jayson said.

"Thank you" I replied.

"We have to celebrate" mommy said.

"Yes we do" Jayson agreed.

And that is exactly what we did for the remainder of the night.

CHAPTER 8

Six Months Later

"I'm in the kitchen bae" Lauren said.

I walked in and there she was standing over the stove looking sexy as shit in her white beater and boy shorts ass just dripping out the bottom.

Damn we had been so caught up these last few weeks with the wedding that I had forgot I ain't had no pussy. Just seeing her made my dick instantly hard.

"Smells good, you smell good too" I said in between the kisses I placed on her neck.

"Stop the food almost done" she said.

"Naw, I want you first" still kissing her neck.

I could tell by the arch in her back she was getting wet that was confirmed when she started turning the stove down on low.

I spun her around lifting her shirt up and began sucking a messaging her titties running my tongue all over her nipples, as they got hard. So I slip my hand in her shorts and start massaging her clit.

"Ahhhh" she moaned softly.

I lifted her up on the counter top and was eye level with her soaking pussy. Quickly placing one leg over my shoulder, I made love to her love box. It wasn't long before baby was moaning and shaking and gliding my head the way she liked so I could please her perfectly.

"Oh shit bae I'm about to cum" she said repeatedly.

So of course I sped up the pace licking and sucking faster.

"oh shit don't stop, right there" she moaned loud.

I sucked every drop of her juices then pulled her down and bent her over the counter spreading her ass apart and slide right into home base. Lifting that ass up and grabbing a fist full of hair I started long stroking wasn't long before she was moaning so loud and telling me she loved me and asking was this her dick.

"You damn right this your dick" I said slapping her ass.

"Yes" she screamed.

"This pussy so good bae and I'm about to cum" I said.

Immediately she pushed me back with her ass and dropped down taking me in her mouth sucking until it started to cum.

"Damn I'm cumin bae" I moaned.

She sucked faster and caught every drop.

Then got up and kissed me and smiled.

"How was your day baby?" she asked.

"Better now" I smiled.

"Cool now let me finish dinner." she laughed.

"Yeah do that" I smacked her ass and walked off to shower.

My mind had been crazy I talked Lauren into moving in which was great but this wedding and this war my niggas are in right now had been the only thing consuming my damn thoughts.

"He is upstairs in his office" I heard Lauren say.

Must've been Mariah so I hurried and finished my

shower.

"Yo" I heard KP voice.

"Oh what's up G. I'm in the shower here I come" I said.

For him to stop by it must be important I thought.

"What's up fam" I said.

"Yo bro, you got problems you know Taylor was over the

crib today snapping about this wedding. Saying how you

didn't even tell her" he said.

"Fo real?" I questioned.

"Yeah man she on that shit saying how Mariah not being

in the wedding and how could you get married after all

yall been through. She was crying and shit. Man I

bounced and came straight over here" he whispered

trying not to let Lauren hear him.

"Man she tripping to be honest I thought Mariah would have mentioned it to her" I said.

"Dude you know Riah not going against you" he replied.

He was right that was my baby girl and she definitely would not put me in a crazy position with her mom.

"What you gonna do" he asked.

"I gotta have a convo with her man damn" I said.

"yeah nigga cause the wedding two weeks away don't want her to crash your shit" he laughed.

That shit was not funny cause that's exactly the type of retarded shit she would do. Yeah I had to handle her ASAP.

"But you ready to say I DO bro" he asked.

"yeah man I'm ready plus this wedding killing a nigga pocket" I laughed.

"I bet. You know you in a new league Lauren is real life high maintenance no faking." He laughed.

"That for damn sure. But baby got some paper stacked believe that" I said.

"oh no doubt" he responded.

"You pick up your tux?' I asked.

"Yep. Yesterday that shit fly too" he said.

"I'm going to get mines tomorrow" I said.

"My nigga about to give up all this pussy we been getting forever to be a family man. I'm proud of you J, you know who would've ever thought a player like you would hang it up so soon" he laughed.

I laughed.

"Man when you find that one nothing else is even worth is anymore" I said sounding all soft.

I ain't gonna lie Lauren is bringing the soft side out of a nigga like damn am I losing my touch or something.

But fuck that I was ready more than ever to be a husband and just live a normal life with my wife and my daughter. I might just get her pregnant the pussy so fucking good.

"Yo tomorrow we opening late, her mom and sister giving her a bridal party or whatever the fuck you call that shit" I said.

"Oh ok, damn is her sister fine? he asked.

"Niggas you a nut, see that why you always in a trouble at the crib" I laughed.

"You right but damn is she nice?" he said a second time.

"Yeah bro she nice but stay your ass away" I cracked up giving him a pound.

"Oh yeah I got office work to do tomorrow anyway so I'll be there" he just smiled and walked out.

Lauren

"It smells good" I heard Mariah say coming through the door.

"Hey sweetie" I said.

"Hey" she gave me a hug.

I was beyond grateful that Mariah and I had a good relationship that was my little boo.

"Let me find out you cook better than dad" she was lifting up the lids to the pots.

"Girl you can't tell him that not Chef Black" we laughed.

"So what's going on you ready for your shower tomorrow and did you ask daddy if I could come" she said.

"It did slip my mind I am sorry I will ask him later, he should be okay with it because it is at the club so he can just watch us on surveillance" I said smiling.

"I hope because I want to come. I am a part of the bride's crew" she said.

"yes you are don't worry I'll handle your dad." I reassured her.

I'll be right back" I said.

I walked into the bedroom.

"Bae" I said.

"I'm right here" he responded from his office.

"Um I forgot to tell you that mom is coming by, we just got to wrap up this wedding stuff and Mariah is downstairs and the food is done" I was talking so fast.

"Come here" he said.

I walked over and sat on the edge of his desk putting my foot on his lap.

"You good?" he asked.

"I'm okay just a little overwhelmed baby" I said.

"Well chill out that why I told you to get a wedding planner" he said.

"Mommy was not having that" I laughed.

"You gotta relax you got everything you wanted and most of all you got me" he said giving me kiss.

"Thank you baby you always make me feel better" I smiled feeling at ease.

"Oh and please let Mariah come to the shower tomorrow she doesn't want to be left out and you know I will make sure she doesn't drink or nothing" I said pleading.

"I don't know" he asked.

"Bae come on its not like you'll be far away anyways" I laughed.

"Alright, now get your spoiled ass out my office" he said smacking my butt.

"Thanks, come eat" I laughed.

I returned to the kitchen Mariah was making plates.

I gave her a wink "you can come" I said.

"Yes" giving me a high five just as her dad was walking in.

"Ya'll not slick" he said.

We all just laughed.

The doorbell rang.

I went to open the door and to my surprise it was Taylor his baby mom and I only knew who she was because I asked to see a picture of her. First I was unsure what to even say but that instantly came to an end when she said.

"Excuse me but can you get Jayson"

Her tone made me want to slap the shit out of her now was not the time.

"Bae I yelled can you come here" I said.

Her face turned so red.

"What's wrong baby" Jayson said walking to the door.

I opened the door wider so he could see.

"Taylor" he was puzzled.

She went ham. "SO YOU JUST GONNA GET MARRIED AND NOT TELL ME AND I DON'T EVEN KNOW THIS BITCH………."

I just walked away when I heard bitch. I was not about to go there with her I was confident that Jayson would handle it.

Mariah started walking to the door clearly hearing her mom's voice.

"AND YALL OVER HERE PLAYING FUCKING HOUSE WITH MY DAUGHTER" Taylor said seeing Mariah.

"Shut the fuck up" Jayson said his voice was so stern.

"I JUST WANT SOME ANSWERS" Taylor said still loud.

"First of all I don't t have to tell you shit but let's go out back and we can talk" he said.

"Damn I can't even come in your house now cause your bitch?' she said.

"Yo, make that your last time saying bitch or we not talking about shit and I mean that" Jayson said.

They walked out back and I was so relived because my mom and London were pulling in the drive way.

"Hey yall" I said meeting them at the door.

"This is a nice ass house" London said giving me a hug.

I was hoping for everyone sake that Taylor would lower her fucking voice and Jayson would handle that so she could leave.

But best believe I would be having a conversation with my "husband" later tonight.

Mariah came back inside shaking her head.

"Oh hi" she said.

"Mariah this is my mom Jackie and my sister London" I said.

"Nice to meet you both" she said giving them hugs.

"You are pretty" They said in unison.

"Thank you, Lauren I am gonna eat my food upstairs and let you talk" she said disappearing I could tell she was embarrassed by her mom. I would talk to her later about it.

"Are you ready for tomorrow" London asked.

"I guess" I said

"You guess? What's wrong with you?" she asked.

Nothing. Just overwhelmed I guess" I said.

"Well everything is under control Lauren so you can relax" said mommy.

"All the dresses will be picked up tomorrow including yours" she said.

"I can't wait to see it finally with all the alterations" I said trying to mask my nervousness.

"Oh where is your soon to be husband anyways" mom asked.

"He is out back handling something he will be in shortly" I responded.

We went over every single detail of this wedding I was so grateful that my mom was handling everything. I was positive that my day would be beautiful. Shay and London had planning this party so I was sure it would be crazy but I needed a little turn up. I had not been able to even fucking breath between this wedding and the office had been booming with new clientele.

Jayson walked in the door and his look confirmed that he had in fact handled Taylor. He came and sat next to me grabbing my hand to ease my mood.

"What did I miss" he asked.

Everything but nothing important for you" mom said laughing.

"Good" he smiled.

"I will have what you asked me tomorrow Mrs. Jackie" he said.

"Great, you can just come by Lauren's then" she responded.

"Deal" he said.

"Mariah is upstairs bae" I said giving him a concerned look.

"Excuse me ladies if I am not needed I'll be back" he said leaving out the living room.

I suggested that we head to the mall to find an outfit for the shower tomorrow that way they could have some privacy.

"Baby I'll be back I'm going to the mall" I yelled up the stairs.

"Ok. Take the card in the drawer and get whatever you want bae" he said back.

I just smiled.

Jayson

"This shit looks good" I whispered to myself. Standing in the mirror with my tux on for the last time before the big day. KP, Mac, my cousin Trey, Jamie and Kyree all had their final fitting today too.

"Fuck that they not having all the fun tonight" Mac said.

"Fucking right" I laughed.

We decided to just throw a big ass party for both of us tonight. Lauren had no problem that I was invading on her bridal thing tonight she was actually happy to have everyone together before the wedding and party.

"You almost ready baby" I asked Lauren

"Almost can you zip me up" she said coming into my closet.

"Damn that's what you wearing" I said my dick getting hard.

"What you don't like it? Is it too much?" she asked.

"man you look good as fuck bae" I said.

My wife was sexy as fuck in this all white two piece tight fitting pants thing. She looked so good I couldn't even put it into words. Her ass was so round a perfect.

"Oh good well zip these pants please" she asked.

As she turned around to for me to zip them up I seen she had on no panties and I couldn't take it I bagan zipping them up but started to rub my dick up against her ass and grabbed her breast from behind.

"BAEEEEEEEE don't start we gotta go we are already late" she said.

"Real quick, fuck them they can wait" I said still rubbing and kissing her neck.

I was already starting to tug at her pants to get them off. I could tell by the way she was squirming that she was getting horny.

"We got all night baby, mom gonna be calling me any minute" she said.

I silenced her by kissing her in the mouth. She of course kissed me back.

I quickly lifted her up and moved back up against the wall.

"Hurry up" she demanded.

"Say no more" I said sliding right into her wetness.

She let out a big gasp and dug her nails into by back.

No letting up I went deeper and deeper beating her walls down.

"Oh my god bae" she moaned.

I had no time to waste so I never stopped. I could feel myself about to bust.

"I'm about to cum" I said.

"Yes me too cum with me" she said. I felt her cumming all over my dick I couldn't hold it. Or pull out.

"Damn" I said.

We both had to shower quickly and get dressed again.

I never seen her move that fast in 20 minutes she was effortlessly beautiful and ready.

"You're gorgeous baby" I complimented her.

"Thank you, and you look damn good yourself daddy" she smiled.

Usually I don't drive the Rolls Royce but tonight was a special occasion.

I opened the door for her and we headed to the club.

When we pulled up it was packed.

"I thought you had closed the club down for tonight?" Lauren asked.

"I bet KP & Mac opened since we said we would do something together. Is that okay? If not I'll make everyone leave" I said.

"No baby its fine as long as we have a good night

tonight?" she replied.

"You sure?" I asked.

"Yes. I'm getting fucked up tonight so we can finish what

we started" she gave me a sexy as smirk.

"Oh well let's get the drinks following quicker you get

drunk the faster we can go home" I laughed.

"Just be able to hang" she laughed.

Funny thing is she is the biggest lightweight I ever met

three shots and she's done.

From the look of the parking lot the whole damn city had

come out and that was confirmed when we stepped

inside. I was hoping Lauren did not really mind because I

know this was supposed to be about her tonight and shit I

learned long ago about the saying happy wife happy life.

 "Damn I'm getting soft," I thought to myself.

Mommy Jackie had it looking really nice in here though and I could tell by the smile on her face that she was cool. Sitting the in section was all our family and friends. The bottles had already begun to flow seeing how we were running late.

"Damn G I thought you wasn't coming" Mac joked dapping me up.

"My wife was fashionable late" I said.

"Oh no don't blame me" she smirked.

"What" I laughed giving her a light tap on the ass.

"See what I mean" Lauren joked.

"Oh get a room" London came over giving us hugs.

London poured us both a glass of champagne and we began to party.

KP had come down from the office.

I introduced him to everyone this was the first time everyone had met before the wedding.

"Jamie and Kyree these are my best friends KP and Mac" I said.

They all dapped and said what's up introducing themselves. I also introduced them to London and Shay and Momma Jackie and a few of Laurens cousins that had come into town.

Lauren's college friend Kya had also came up and surprised her.

She seemed like a thorough ass bitch her energy was 100% New York but from her turn up and conversation, she was cool.

What I did notice was KP and Kyree something was up both of them frequently side eyed the other.

"Yo K let me holler at you" I said pulling him to the side.

"What's good?" he said.

"You good fam you seem off" I asked. He knew what I was getting at.

"I don't know seem like I know old boy from somewhere or something" he said referring to Kyree.

"You sure?" I asked.

"Not 100% but the way he keep looking at me makes me think I'm kinda right" he said.

"Well for the sake of tonight keep cool" I said.

"You know better G plus I still ain't put my finger on it but I will" he said.

He lifted his glass to minds and threw his shot back. I did the same.

Whatever was on K's mind we could worry about it tomorrow.

Lauren was so turnt dancing with her friend and Mariah I was happy she was enjoying herself she needed it after all the stress from work and the wedding. Seeing the way her a Mariah's relationship had been blooming made me happy. These were the two most important woman in my life. I walked over to her wrapping my arms around her back.

She started dancing on me and singing. She was undeniably drunk and it was cute.

I was so distracted by my baby that I didn't even notice until it was too fucking late.

POW POW POW POW POW POW !

Was all I heard I instantly grabbed her and Mariah down to the floor. I reached for my gun and realized where I was that I didn't have it. I never carried my gun in my own club because my security was extra tight. I looked around and seen the glimpse of the niggas running out of the club. I looked around and I didn't see Kyree. Something struck me odd. Everyone was rushing the exits I needed to get downstairs immediately. I walked Lauren, Riah and her family to my office, grabbed my gun and locked the door.

I headed to main entrance and in the back hallway, I heard a commotion so I slowly headed that way but they must've heard my shoes coming because by the time I turned the corner they were running out the exit.

I did manage to hear "you ain't kill that nigga?

But I didn't recognize the voice.

They had to be some stupid muthafuckas though. I had the best surveillance cameras so I would be able to see everything.

We cleared the club and of course, the police and shit showed up. I did not even want to deal with that so I let Keisha handle that. I trusted her and she knew what and what not to say. I headed up to the office and KP was inside but his expression told me he needed to talk.

Lauren was looking like what the fuck. But I am sure it was because her mom was there. I immediately apologized.

"This never happens here. We don't even have that type of crowd" I said looking at Mrs. Jackie.

"Baby you can't control everything I understand" she said.

"Baby you okay to drive home or would you like me to have someone take you" I asked.

"I'll drive us" she said.

"You okay baby girl" I said to Riah kissing her on the forehead. She was a little shook up I could tell. Mariah was not so street she knew things but not that much.

"I got her" Lauren said.

"Thank you" I kissed them both, KP and I walked them to the front, and valet had pulled up my car.

"Go straight home, I'll be there soon as I can" I closed the door.

I was furious but I didn't want to spazz in front of the babies.

"What the fuck is going on K" I said.

"Yo how the fuck did them niggas get a strap in here," he said back.

"That's what the fuck I'm trying to figure out" I said.

"We gotta watch the cameras," he said.

"Right fucking now," I said.

"I got a funny feeling about this shit" KP mumbled.

He was right something didn't make sense this wasn't your neighborhood ghetto ass bar this was the biggest, newest club in the whole city.

In the office we both sat in front of the monitor and replayed the entire nights video. I noticed a group of bitches come in and a nigga behind them but he slide by the bitch never got searched and slide right the fuck past the metal detectors. The nigga was real fucking black and he had on all black but he didn't look familiar at all. On the other monitor in the sections we seen us and I zoomed in cause it was almost as if soon as the nigga walked in Kyree had got up and we aint see that nigga all night. Where the fuck did he go? What kinda nigga leave his mom and sister in the club while they shooting? I thought all this but I didn't say nothing. I seen KP thinking but he didn't say nothing either but I knew my nigga so well I'm sure we was on the same page.

I called down to Keisha "tell big Rob get the fuck up here now"

Rob was the head of fucking security so this shit falls on him.

"What the fuck happened how the fuck niggas get in my shit with straps?" I said as calm as possible.

I tried to have some respect and not knock this niggas the fuck out.

"My muthafucking daughter and wife was here tonight" I said a little louder cause I was getting madder by the fucking minute.

"I checked everyone that came through" he said.

"No the fuck you didn't I'll show you" I said.

KP ran the tape back and there was Big Rob distracted by these bitches and dude slide right the fuck past.

"So you mean to tell me these nappy headed hoes had you that distracted that you let that shit happen"

"Um um um man I don't know," he said.

"Well since you don't fucking know and you don't have no explanation to this dumb shit you ain't even gotta worry about coming back cause you can't be unaware" I said.

"Come on Jay it was a mistake it was so busy and..." he started to say

"No that's no excuse" I cut him off in mid- sentence now please get out my office.

Big Rob got up and just walked out because he knew that I wasn't gonna repeat myself and if I didn't it wasn't gonna be this nice.

"What we need to figure out is who the fuck that nigga was and where the fuck did your brother in law go?" KP said.

He was absolutely right.

"I know you all family man and want to keep the peace but I need you all in on this one" he said.

"No doubt" I said.

"I'll catch you later," he said leaving.

"FUCK" I yelled.

KP sat in his car and just thought, "I don't trust that nigga man" he said aloud rubbing his head.

He knew something was up and he just hoped that this wedding and the exit from the streets wasn't affecting his man's judgement.

This nigga in love but love will get you fucking killed.

KP was used to Jayson being on his mark but it was clear that his mind was clouded so he knew he had to be extra aware as to what was going on.

Lauren:

"What the fuck was that about" I thought to myself and more importantly what was the odds of it happening on the night of our wedding parties.

Stress was an understatement.

"Hey have you talked to my dad?" Mariah asked.

"No not yet I didn't want to bother him" I responded.

"Are you okay?" I asked.

"Yes, are you?" she said.

"Yes I'm fine. Mariah, are you okay with your dad and I getting married. I mean I know your mom was really upset and I'm not trying to be your mom or anything like that but I just want to know how you really feel," I said.

"Lauren I love you and my dad. I wouldn't want him to marry anyone else. My mom is okay that's just how she is don't sweat it too much." She said smiling.

"Great well I hate that happened tonight because we were having such a good time" I said.

"Yeah it was fun, and your mom be jamming" she laughed.

"Girl she is something" I laughed.

"Well I'm gonna call it a night just please check on my dad" she asked.

"Let's call him now" I said dialing his number.

"Hello" he said.

"Hey babe it's me and Mariah are you okay?" I asked.

"Yes I'm good I'm headed home now," he said.

"Okay love you dad," said Mariah.

"I love you more" he said hanging up.

"Good night" Mariah gave me a hug.

"Good night sweetie" I hugged her back.

It wasn't long before I heard Jayson coming in. He came into the living room and kissed me.

"I am sorry about all that" he apologized.

"It's not your fault and I'm fine bae, are you okay?" I asked.

"I'm cool yet gotta get ahold on all this shit" he said.

"I don't want you to be mad about me asking but I have to" he said.

"Go ahead" I said.

"Where did your brother go tonight?" I asked.

I kinda was wondering why he asked but honestly that was the same question I had in my head all night and I still had not talked to him. Jamie had taken mommy and London to my house so I knew his whereabouts but where the fuck was Kyree.

"Honestly bae I been wondering the same I'm not sure" I said.

"Do you think he had beef with any people up this way?" he asked.

"I really don't know he tells me shit but not much when it comes to that kind of stuff "I said.

"Oh okay" he said.

I could tell something was bothering him but I did not want to press the issue.

"Well so much for our drunk sex" I said to lighten the mood.

"Yeah I'm completely sober now," he laughed.

"Shit me too" I said.

"That don't mean I can't break your back down if that's

what you on" he said kissing me.

"Mariah is still up" I whispered.

"Lucky you" he said walking off to check on her.

I was not in any mood to be having sex. This was

supposed to be a very happen night for us and Thank

God, no one was hurt. That is not at all, what we need.

However, if I knew anything I knew Jayson would handle

it and I knew he would protect my career but the funny

thing is I wasn't even worried about that so much any

more. I wanted my husband to be worry free and now I

was starting to get the impression that his recent stress

had not been from the wedding.

CHAPTER 9

THREE WEEKS LATER

Jayson:

I was always taught men don't cry but damn she was like a goddess walking down that aisle. I knew that she was heaven sent that very night she walked into the club. Her smile showed the purest love and true beauty from the inside. I couldn't fight back the tears at all. I had waited for this moment all my life to marry a queen, someone I didn't have to question or second-guess and that just loved me for me not for what I could provide. My OG told me a man that finds a wife finds a good thing, I had found my wife, and everything about Lauren was good. Finally she had made it to the alter I reached out and grabbed her hand. She smiled and whispered I love you. I whispered it back.

There we stood hand in hand looking in each other's eyes. The preacher gave his word and Lauren began saying her vows "I Lauren Young take you Jayson Black to be my lawfully wedded husband. Jayson you came into my life and gave me a reason to love again, you have made me the happiest woman in the world. You are loving, caring and so amazing I never trusted a human being the way that I trust you. You asked me to give you my heart and you have guarded it with your life. You are everything a real man should be and I stand her today before God and our family to confess my love for you and to let you know that I will love you for always. Through the good and the bad, rich or poor, sickness and in health from this day forward I will be your partner whatever you lack I will be right there to make sure you get back on track baby. You will never be alone another day in this lifetime as I will be there for always until death do us apart and even at that point I will be there in eternal life to love you forever."

"I Jayson Black take you Lauren Young to be my lawfully wedded wife to love and protect for the rest of this lifetime. You are everything man could dream of in a wife and represent all that a woman should be. You are strong, faithful and full of life. The grace and beauty that you display in everything you do is simply amazing, from the very day I seen you and you made me stalk you I knew you were the one. I knew I wanted my soul next to yours forever. I promise to be everything you need as your husband, friend and life partner. I will protect and provide as long as there is breathe in my body. I realize that although I had everything most people desire I really had nothing until the day you came into my life. I love you Lauren and I stand here today making these vows to you and I will never ever break them"

There was not a dry eye in the church every word I spoke I meant. I turned to KP and took the ring Lauren was shocked when she realized I had upgraded her already big ass ring to an even bigger one. I kiss my bride and like that I had become a complete man. Nothing else mattered in that moment but that my baby was happy and that made me happy.

Lauren:

I could not have asked for a more perfect wedding every single detail was immaculate and it was dripping diamonds everywhere. My husband was so fine standing there and I was shocked to see him shed a tear. He is so sweet and now I was finally Mrs. Black. Only thing missing was my dad and because he was absent I didn't have anyone give me away because no one could ever fill his shoes. I loved my brothers but they were not my dad.

We decided not to ride in the party bus and we got in the car and had a moment to ourselves before the turn up began. We drove to the very first place we had ever gone on a date it we parked and got out and just walked for a moment. I took his hand and we walked neither of us said anything we just looked at each other a smiled. The silence was worth more than 1,000 words. I knew he loved me and I loved him. How did I get so luck I was unsure but I was grateful. After we took our walk, we headed back to the car we still needed to meet the wedding party for photos and then we had the reception and I still needed to change into my second dress.

"I love you" he said as he began lifting up my dress.

"Bae you are not supposed to see under this dress until later" I laughed.

"I don't follow rules baby I'm a boss but you knew that" he smiled hands on my pussy at this point.

"Just untraditional" I teased.

"You sure are wet for someone that's talking about tradition" he replied.

I must admit seeing my husband in his tux was so fucking sexy and his touch always did something to my body.

I let out a soft moan "ummmmmm" and just that fast my panties were to the side and with his thumb on my clit and index finger inside my pussy he went in. He never took his hand eyes off the road as I came all over his fingers and seat. We pulled up to the Sherton Hotel and got out like nothing had happened. We made our grand entrance for the first time ever as Mr. & Mrs. Black and there was everyone standing and clapping. The DJ played Jay- Z & Beyonce "On the Run Part II" and   nothing could change the happiness I felt. Jayson wasn't much of a dancer but he held my hand and let me do my thing. He grabbed me close and did a little two step and from that moment we never stopped partying. Our reception was so lit and of course my mother and sister made me cry with their speeches but the best speech of the night was KP. The bond and love that he Jayson shared showed so much today. You can tell that he was proud of the man his brother had become. He thanked me for making his man so happy. It was a beautiful speech and I even think I seen my baby shed another tear. After what seemed like the longest day ever it was finally over. Our guests began to leave and my mom was, making sure everything was being taken care of so we decided to head to our hotel everyone begged us to come out but we just wanted to enjoy our night as husband and wife, plus I was drunk and very ready to go consummate my marriage. Just as we were leaving, Mariah and KP stopped us.

"Daddy, Uncle K gonna take me to the house are you guys coming home tonight?" Mariah asked.

"No baby we gonna stay overnight at the hotel" Jayson said.

"Ok now don't make a baby" she laughed.

"Oh NO" I cut in laughing.

Mariah gave both of us hugs and said she was so happy and that today was so beautiful.

"Tomorrow we will have brunch and talk all about it and look at some pictures" I said.

"Aight Bro we out I'm taking Raih to the crib and I'm gonna hit the club shit a nigga looking good in this tux" KP said.

"Aight bro love you" Jayson said.

"Love you too bro, congratulations man ya'll did that shit" he said smiling.

"Now it's your turn," I said.

"Yeah not yet sis, not yet" he laughed.

Mariah

"I'm really happy for my dad Uncle K" I said.

"I am too Lauren is good for him" said Uncle KP.

"You sure you gonna be okay in the house by yourself?" he asked.

"I am not a baby anymore Uncle K but I'm so tired I'll be sleep in 10 minutes" I laughed.

"I don't want to hear that you will always be my little Riah" he joked pinching my cheeks.

I had been around Uncle KP all my life whenever my dad could not do something he was always there to do it. He was like my second dad and I could talk to him about any and everything.

We turned onto our block uncle K turned the music down it was late and it was already hard being the only black people in the neighborhood so we never wanted to draw to much attention. Suddenly it was a loud crash, a car had blasted us from behind pushing us into the pole. Two men got out and in all black and masks. Uncle K grabbed his gun and began shooting. One of the guys came up and grabbed me pointing the gun in my face. I always remembered my dad telling me to just pay attention and try and remember anything about them. At that point I stopped panicicking and tries to hear their voices, see the skin color, anything but that all came to a hault when…… BOOM, BOOM, BOOM.

"Uncle K" I screamed.

My life flashed before my eyes as the one guy had the gun pointed at me ready to shoot.

"Hell naw let her live and tell the story," the other guy said.

They both ran off down the street getting in a different car and driving off.

"Uncle K" I began pressing his chest applying some pressure.

"DON'T DIE PLEASE DON'T DIE" I repeated over and over.

"call your da" Uncle K managed to say.

I called 911 and then immediately began calling my dad back to back to back but he wasn't answering and my dad always answered. I began to panic had someone killed my dad and Lauren.

"Breathe Uncle K. I hear help, they are coming," I said holding him in my lap.

"I love you Riah I'm okay," he said.

"Ok. Don't talk Uncle K just breathe" I said.

The ambulance finally arrived and it was complete chaos they began ripping his clothes off, blood was everywhere; they thought I was shot also. There were about 10 police cars and I was overwhelmed I felt myself drifting and everything went black.

Jayson

"Yes, yes, yes bae yes" Lauren screamed digging her nails in my back as I licked and sucked on her clit just they was she liked it.

Just as I could feel her legs shaking uncontrollably my phone began ringing but whoever was calling would have to wait.

"Don't stop daddy, don't stop," she moaned louder and louder.

I got up to enter and she pushed me and back a slide right down on my throbbing dick. I gripped her ass and helped her glide up and down.

"Damn ride that dick Mrs. Black," I said smacking her ass.

One thing about her is when she is drunk she has the most stamina and she gets wetter than the ocean.

"I'm cumming" she moaned.

But she didn have to tell me because I felt it. "Fuck" I said.

But my phone just kept ringing causing Lauren to stop instantly.

Who keeps calling" she said with a small attitude.

"I don't know let me just put it on silent ill call them back tomorrow.

I picked up my phone and seen it was Mariah calling then Taylor and then some number I didn't recognize. My face must have given it away.

"What's wrong baby?" Lauren asked.

I didn't answer her I called Mariah and got no answer so I called Taylor but she was so hysterical that I couldn't really make out what she was saying other than get here

now we are at St. Elizabeth Hospital.

"We gotta go I don't know what happened but Taylor is

at the hospital I don't know let's go" I said putting on my

pants and shirt.

Lauren jumped up and began putting on her dress and we

rushed to the hospital.

I knew something was wrong when we arrived because it

was too many cars that I recognized so I rushed in and I

seen Taylor crying.

"What the fuck happened where is Mariah" I yelled.

Then I seen her covered in blood and crying in the chair.

"What the fuck" I said.

Daddy they shot him, they hit us and they shot him, I held

him but they shot him" Mariah was so upset and shaking.

I held my baby and told her it was okay I knew she was

in no shape to tell me what was wrong.

The feeling I had going through my body was fucking indescribable. Who the fuck was crazy enough to pull this shit in front of my daughter? Before I could speak to anyone the doctor came from behind the doors and I knew by his expression it wasn't good but my brain didn't register any words after hearing him say "I'm sorry...... Mr. Perkins didn't make it"

The hospital went in a rage but my legs wouldn't move, the words wouldn't come out my mouth, I felt Lauren's hand touch my back but it was Taylor's mouth that snapped my daze.

"Bitch you don't even know him like that" she said to Lauren.

Lauren just looked at her shocked.

"Do you even know his real name yes bitch KP stands for Ke"Mari Perkins did you know that hell naw. You been around for a second you shouldn't even be here hoe. You don't even know your own husband like that bitch" she

went on and on.

"Taylor shut the fuck up, now is not the time" I grabbed

her arm pushing her into the chair

"Get off of me" she yelled.

"You fucking tripping, bitch our daughter just seen her

uncle get shot and you talking about Lauren" I said.

I just walked off. I wanted to see my brother even though

my mind was racing I just couldn't believe it until I seen

him.

I found the doctor and asked him to let me back in the

room to see K.

"Sir only family can..." he began to say.

"I am his brother," I said cutting him off.

When I got to the door, I couldn't believe my eyes my

brother, my friend was laid up bloody under a white sheet

DEAD. Damn I couldn't hold back the tears I dropped to

his side and cried. I never cried so hard in my entire life.

How the fuck did this happen? How did the happiest day

of my life turn into the worst day of my life?

"I'm gonna murk them niggas K or die trying" I walked

out of the room I had seen enough.

My daughter was traumatized I had managed to keep this

gangster shit from her all her life but now she would have

to carry this with her forever.

I found Lauren and Mariah sitting outside the hospital

talking. I felt bad for my wife because Taylor was right

she didn't really know who I used to be but she was about

to find out. I was about to paint this muthafuckin city red

until I found out who did this.

Lauren:

What the fuck was going on I thought riding home.

Jayson's expression was something I had never seen

before and Mariah was a wreck in the back seat. My

wedding dress had blood from hugging Mariah it was all just a mess and I couldn't believe that KP was really dead. How did the best day of my life turn into such a tragedy something just didn't seem right in my gut but maybe I was just upset and seeing my husband hurting was breaking my heart. The ride home was silence and long but once we arrived I knew that Jayson wasn't staying. He kissed me and Mariah and was out the door just as fast as we came in.

"Please be careful" I said as he left.

But he didn't respond and he was gone that fast.

I felt safe at home we had the best security cameras and you needed the code to the gate to get in.

Mariah was upstairs in the shower and I could hear her sobbing funny thing is I knew exactly what she was feeling because I had seen murder with my own eyes and it is disturbing to the mind. Mariah was so innocent, sweet this was the type of things that turned good girls into heartless monsters, and I didn't want that for my stepdaughter. When she got out the shower, I knocked on her door.

"Hey" I said.

She looked at me and just dropped her head.

"Its ok baby" I said hugging her and rubbing her hair

"Come get in the bed with me, I don't want you sleeping alone and I don't want to sleep alone.

We went and got in the bed and Mariah cuddled in my arms. I prayed a powerful prayer and rubbed her back. I cried and prayed and cried some more. Eventually Mariah drifted off to sleep and it wasn't soon after that I must've fallen asleep too because it was the sun coming through the windows that woke me. Mariah was still asleep and she needed it so I didn't move I laid and drifted back into sleep for a little while longer. The nonstop ringing of the phone is what woke me and although I

knew everyone just wanted to make sure I was okay I just

didn't feel like talking. I noticed my husband had not

been home nor had he called. I was so worried about him

I called his phone but got no answer but just as I was

leaving a voicemail. I received a text

Hubby: I am ok. I love you.

Me: Thank you, I love you more.

I was relieved that he was okay but I know what this pain

can do to a person's mind and heart. It was like living in a

nightmare and I could not wrap my head around the pain

I knew Jayson was feeling. Not even my love for him

coud cure that but I would do my best as his wife to make

it easier to cope.

I heard Mariah getting up and heading down the stairs she

came into the kitchen

"Hey" she said

~ 250 ~

"Hey sweetheart" I replied grabbing her hand.

"My dad still gone?" she asked.

"Yes but he just texted me the he was ok" I said I did not need her worrying about her dad.

"Lauren I think I'm just gonna stay here with you guys, my mom works a lot and it's just safe here and I don't know.." she rambled.

"Of course, this is your home too and I am on vacation for a few weeks so you won't be alone" I smiled.

"I am so sorry your wedding day was ruined" she apologized.

"Oh hunny don't you be sorry for anything, you had no control over yesterday and although the ending was tragic I still married my best friend and it was beautiful" I responded.

LOVE OR LOYALTY

"You truly are a beautiful person Lauren I am glad my dad found you. He needs you more than ever now" she said looking me in the eyes.

"I got him and you too" I said giving her that reassurance she needed.

She smiled and walked back upstairs.

Mariah:

The shower still had not washed away this feeling I had although the blood was gone it still seemed to stain my body. I could vision the life leaving Uncle K's body. I sobbed quietly in the shower and prayed. I knew it was about to get dangerous and I was afraid of that. Lauren or my dad knew just how much I really knew about what my dad got into. I knew so much, I heard so much and whenever my mom felt like I was loving him more than her she let me know just how much of a street nigga he was. I knew my dad had killed people before and I knew that my dad had the biggest bag in the city. Therefore, it wasn't just by chance that I lived better than most of the rich white kids at my school. We always lived in a nice house, drove nice cars and I had every designer in my closet. The type of things you see in the movies and read in books but to me he was just dad because he never bought any of that around me, I only knew these things from hearing my mom talk and eavesdropping on conversations my dad had with Uncle K. I was scared though because I knew that my dad was going to kill someone and I didn't want to lose my dad to jail or have someone kill him. I knew he was hurt about Uncle K but I also knew he was more hurt that I was in the cross fire and he wasn't there to protect me. What I didn't understand was why this was happening to my family. I showered until I heard a knock at the door.

"Baby girl" I heard my dad say.

"Hold on" I go out and dried off.

"Come in" I said once I had my robe on.

My dad came in and sat on the toilet, we locked eyes. He was hurting and that hurt me so bad to see him this way.

"You ok" I asked hugging him.

"Not really, what about you" he said.

"Not really, but we will be" I said hugging him.

We just hugged no word and that was okay my dad brought comfort and protection to my life that no one would ever understand.

"You eat" he asked breaking the silence.

"No, but Lauren did say she would make me something after I showered.

"Yes, she making something now" he said.

"She wonderful" I said smiling.

He smiled.

I didn't have much of an appetite but my stomach said otherwise.

Jayson:

Mac and I had been up all night trying to figure out what the fuck was up. The series of events just didn't make sense, what did K have going on outside of what he was telling us. Man K told me everything and something just wasn't right he didn't mention anything serious enough to have him murked.

One thing for sure though I can't react right now they will see me coming whoever the fuck they was. I was coming that was for sure but they had to know that so for now I'll just wait and pay attention to everything around me.

I should be on my honey moon right now but I gotta bury my fucking brother. I couldn't describe the pain and I wasn't ready to face it at all I thought sitting outside his mom crib. It had hit me like a ton of bricks seeing

everyone gathered and bringing food and crying and shit.

Soon as I entered the door everyone looked, shit this was

like my family too Ms. Karen was more of a mother to

me then my mom growing up. She was in her room. I

knocked before going in.

"Hey baby come in" she patted the bed next to her.

I sat down and she cried a little.

"What happened" she asked.

"I really don't know but I will find out" I said it pissed

me off that I truly didn't have an answer.

"Promise me you won't get yourself killed I can't handle

two dead son's" she said looking at me.

"I can't tell you a lie Momma Karen" I said.

She grabbed my hand and squeezed it tight.

"You are a married man now Jayson you owe it to her to stay alive and Mariah adores you she needs her dad, ok baby" she said.

"Yes" I said.

"Oh, and the wedding was stunning I never seen you smile so hard" she laughed.

"Thank you, she's the best thing that happened to me and you know everything will be handled just let me know the total I'll drop it off" I said.

"I know baby I know," she said giving me a hug.

I had knew where all K's money was and what to do if anything ever happened but damn I never ever thought anything would happen. FUCK!!!!

Lauren:

"Bae I'm so sorry" I said as he held me tight. Just being in my his arms made me feel okay. He kissed my forehead.

"Not how I expected to spend our first few nights being married" he said.

"Right but it's okay because we have forever to go" I said.

"Thank You" he said.

"You want to pray?" I asked.

He sat up in the bed and looked at me.

"What's wrong?" I asked.

He sat there for another moment.

"No one has ever asked me that?" he said.

"To pray?" I asked.

"I never been that close to a woman" he said.

I grabbed his hand.

"Close your eyes"

He did.

I prayed.

It was calming something we both needed. We sat in bed and just talked listening to him talk about how he grew up and his memories with him and KP just the things they used to do. We just laughed at some of the stories.

"Oh you was just a little hoe" I said.

"Damn wife, its like that?" he laughed.

I knew he was hurting but that brief moment of laughter was good for him.

The next few days were very hard but we made it through the funeral. The love that KP had received was beautiful. He looked peaceful but not like the brother, I had grown to know. Just wish I had more time to get to know him. Of course, everyone watched Jayson looking for his reaction. I could tell he was doing his best to keep it all together. The service went well and we made it safely to the cemetery. They did the small service, released the Doves and everyone slowly made their way to their cars.

Jayson and Ms. Karen remained sitting waiting for them to place K into the ground. I would give them their moment and wait in the car. As I turned to walk away I felt a hand tap my shoulder. I turn around.

"We got off to a rough start but Mariah really likes you, you are his wife now and I will respect you as such" Taylor said holding out her hand for me to shake.

"No problem Taylor" I extended my hand shaking hers.

We went our separate ways. I didn't trust that bitch something was up but right now was not the time but if she gets out of line I would put her ass right in her place cause she had used all her free passes.

Jayson finally came to the car. He was quiet. He was sad. We drove to Ms. Karen's house.

"We don't have to stay long I just need to drop something off" he said.

"Ok. I am fine just needed to rest my feet these shoes are the devil and I wanted to give you guys a moment that's all" I said.

"As much as they cost they shouldn't hurt," he said.

"Who you telling I'll be grateful for the day they make heels that don't hurt" I laughed.

"Cause we both know your boujee butt not gonna stop wearing them" he laughed.

"You gonna stop calling me boujee, you know your wife so well though" I smiled.

"I do, and I love her" he leaned over and kissed me.

He got out and opened my door like usual. Even during his moment of grief, he still managed to be a perfect gentleman.

We went in the house it was full of people and lots of woman I could tell by the looks on some of their faces that Jayson had slept with them. They had a look of disappointment seeing me right by his side. I am sure they were hoping to catch him at his vulnerable state and comfort him.

I just smiled and said hello to everyone.

Jayson was mingling so I found Ms. Karen in the kitchen she was strong woman reminded me a lot of my mom.

She was just straightening up but I could tell she was tired so I jumped in and helped.

"Baby you don't have to do that I got it" she said.

"It's the least I can do just sit down" I said taking over washing the dishes.

We just talked and the suddenly she got quiet.

I turned around her and Jayson were just smiling.

"You ready" he said.

"Yes" she said.

"Bae, I'm gonna steal her for just a minute," he said.

"Ok. Ill finish up these dishes" I said.

By the time they came back, I was just in my zone cleaning up. I had put up the food so Ms. Karen could just lie down after everyone left.

"Thank you so much," said Ms. Karen announcing her presence.

"None needed," I said giving her a hug and kiss.

"I'll keep praying for your strength," I whispered in her ear.

She gave me a tight hug.

"If you need to get out we can always go shopping asking Jayson it's my favorite," I laughed.

"Oh boy, I think you met your match," she said.

"This can't be good for my credit card," Jayson laughed.

I was happy to finally be home today was long, sad and draining.

Mariah had gone home with Taylor; Jayson laid on the bed and dozed off.

I began to run a bath but decided to just take a shower the

way I was feeling I could fall asleep in the tub. I let the

water hit my body and tried to clear my mind so much

had happened and damn I hadn't even had a moment to

be married. I looked down at my huge ring in admiration.

I closed my eyes.

The bathroom door opening startled me a little. I peeked

my head out and Jayson was undressing getting ready to

join me.

"You scared me babe," I said.

"Sorry, why you let me fall asleep" he stepped in the

shower.

"You needed it" I said.

"Hand me the soap," he asked grabbing my washcloth out

my hand.

He then started washing my back nice and slow. My

arms, neck and legs followed.

"Turn around" he said.

I did and he washed my stomach, breast and feet lifting one leg at a time. He spread my legs washing my thighs and all in between my legs. Standing up he kissed my neck and then my lips. He turned me around grabbing my waist and entering from behind without warning slowly. My pussy was very inviting as I let out a soft moan. After a few long strokes he sped up the pace lifting up one leg and balancing my hands up against the shower wall.

"Oh God" was all I could say. I was caught up in complete ecstasy as my husband beat my walls down clearly releasing his emotions on my pussy but it felt so good. He never slowed down, I moaned louder, and louder it didn't matter because he wasn't stopping. He smacked my ass and wrapped his hands in my hair. He grabbed my head back…..

"Who pussy is this?" he moaned.

"Youuurrrssss" I tried to say in between strokes.

"What I can't hear you" pushing deeper and faster.

"Yours baby, it's your pussy" I screamed.

"Fuck" he moaned.

"I'm about to cum" I said.

"Me too" he pounded.

We both came. Showered and I immediately began

talking shit.

"Now who told you to interrupt my shower" I smirked.

"Oh now you wanna say something you was just

moaning and shit talking about this my pussy?" he

laughed.

"Shut up" I said smacking his arm.

We got in bed and clearly both exhausted we fell asleep

in each other's arms.

Unknown:

If she ever found out about this it would break her heart I thought getting ready to meet with him this shit had gone too far but it was too late I was in way too deep......

Jayson:

Nothing was adding up, No harm had come my way and this made it clear that what happened to K was personal and not business. I was trying to live as normal as possible I didn't really know that losing my brother affect me so badly. Even coming to the club was hard we built this shit together it didn't even feel right anymore, honestly I was thinking about selling. K was the face of the club he made sure we kept the celebrities, the baddest hosts and he kept this muthafucka lit at all times. My heart just wasn't into it anymore. Shit my heart wasn't into anything lately. I haven't even been being a good husband and Lauren had been my light at the end of the tunnel.

The FEDS had tried to investigate the business after KP was killed but that failed we had the best accountant and our books and business dealing on paper were always clean and straight. So I wasn't to pressed about that for the first time ever I could honestly say the FEDS couldn't touch me I was a clean man and damn it felt good.

The only solid information that had surfaced was the hit on KP wasn't local they were some OT niggas but my patience was running low I needed these niggas dead. ASAP!

It was about 12:15pm and I decided to pop up on Lauren it was lunchtime so I would just surprise her.

I made a quick stop grabbing some yellow roses her favorite, when I reached the reception area of course they just told me to go back to her office she was in there.

Baby was so focused on typing she never looked up until I said "excuse me miss"

"Oh hey" she looked up cheesing.

"Hey beautiful" I said.

"Are those for me?" she asked pointing at the roses.

"Idk, there is a card here tho" I teased.

She got up and gave me a hug a kiss then grabbing the flowers out my hand and smelling them she read the card smiling.

"Thank you, I love you. So what brings you by baby?" she asked.

"I just wanted to see you, I know I been slacking lately but I appreciate you," I said grabbing her close and gripping her ass.

"It's ok, did you eat?" she said in between kisses.

"Naw, you?" I asked.

"Nope you wanna grab something actually I can be done for the day if you don't have anything else to do" she said.

"Yeah we can grab something and then go watch a movie or something. I'll watch one of them shows you like to watch and I can rub on your butt" I laughed gripping her ass again.

"You so nasty" she laughed.

I loved that my baby was a boss she could really move how she wanted. Yes, I provided her with whatever she wanted but she had her own she didn't really need me and that was the sexiest shit ever.

"Leave your car here and Ill drop you off in the morning" I said.

"Fine with me, I don't feel like driving" she said.

We stopped grabbed our food and headed to the house. The best thing we had was the ability to just talk about anything and everything. We laughed the whole way home she was so damn silly man.

Lauren:

It seemed to be one thing after another, my mom had been sick lately so I decided to fly home for the weekend and make sure she had all she needed. Jayson had been in better spirits lately so I felt comfortable enough to leave him for just a few days.

Jamie was picking me up from the airport he was usually never available and Kyree comes but he wasn't answering his phone so my big brother saved the day.

"Baby sister" I immediately recognized the voice as I picked up my bag from the conveyer belt.

"JJ" I gave him a big hug. He grabbed my bags and we headed to the car.

"How's mommy?" I asked. I knew Jamie would be straight up with me.

"She's okay sis you know Ma she take care of everyone and everything but herself. She's gonna be happy you are here you know she really miss having you around. Shit I miss having you around just your energy sis" Jamie said.

"I know. I miss you guys too we have to see each other more" I said.

"How is married life? You know I am happy for you baby Jayson a good dude and you deserve that," Jamie said.

"It's really great bro, I was nervous at first but he is the best husband anyone could ask for truly. I mean he's been down since what happened he will be okay," I said.

"Hell yeah that's fucked up man but yeah he gonna be good he has a great woman sis and that's all he needs real shit. I'm proud of you kid" he said

Once we got to the house Jamie let me out he said he would be back he had something to do. I grabbed my bags and went inside. Mommy was in the bed sleeping so I didn't wake her I would shower and get settled.

London was watching TV.

"Hey sister" I said kissing her cheek.

"Hey babe, you made it how was your flight?" she asked.

"A little longer than usual I'm tired and mommy sleep so I'm gonna shower and take a nap" I said.

"Ok, Ky up there" she said.

"Oh fuck him he's been ignoring my calls all week" I said.

"What he never ignored you it's usually me "she laughed.

"It okay I'm about to knock his ass right out" I said heading up stairs.

Ky had the door open to the den he talking to someone but what he was saying didn't make any sense my mouth just dropped I could believe what I was hearing.

"What the fuck" I said startled him.

He turned around and seemed nervous as to just how much of his conversation I had heard. Everything made sense now he had been acting so different lately and I thought maybe he was just stressed but now hearing this I just didn't know what to say.

"You wouldn't understand sis" he said.

"Well help me fucking understand" I said with enough bass in my voice he knew I was serious.

"I never wanted to put you in the middle of this shit Lauren" he said.

"But your still not saying a damn thing I need to know what the fuck happened. I said.

"Street shit man and he had to be handled" Kyree said so coldly.

"So you're telling me that you killed him? How the fuck could you do something like that? Jayson's daughter was there Ky. What the fuck is up with you?" I asked just so confused.

"Just mind your fucking business don't act like you don't know how I get down cause you aint asking no question when I handled Deshawn" he said.

"What the fuck are you for real?" I just could not believe he was hitting that below the belt.

"You are asking me to look at my husband everyday while he hurts knowing the truth" I yelled.

"What the fuck you mean? I'm not asking you to do shit. Fuck that nigga I'm your fucking blood you just married homie. Don't forget what's real" he yelled back.

"Oh my God Ky I can't believe this shit and on my wedding night how could you do that to me?" I asked.

"It wasn't supposed to happen like that but shit happens. Stop acting like you forgot where and what you come from Lauren. All that smart and uppity shit made you forget the family you come from. You may have changed your name to Black but you will always be a fucking Young" he spat.

"What is going on up here" London came in the door.

"Nothing yo muthafucking sister trippin" He said walking away.

London looked confused. I just put up my hand, shook my head, and stormed out.

All I know is I needed to get back home ASAP and find out just how much information my Jayson had knew. This was fucking crazy and the beginning of a bunch of bullshit that I would be right in the middle of. I could just never escape the drama, the pain and hurt just when I thought I was happy.

One thing for sure is I couldn't let Jayson find out.

PERIOD.

THREE DAYS LATER

Jayson:

Lauren's flight got in today she would be home any minute. I heard the garage door open.

"Husband" she said coming in the house.

"In here baby" I said

She jumped in my arms giving me kisses and hugs.

"I missed you" she said.

"I missed you too baby, how mom doing and everyone else?"

"She's doing okay she just needs to not over work herself," she said.

"I'm happy you're back," I said looking into her eyes.

"Me too" she said looking back in my eyes.

Damn she was breaking my heart she wasn't gonna tell me.

She never knew that she had pocket dialed me and that I had heard everything she and her bitch ass brother had argued about.

Damn how could she keep it from me. I trusted her with my life, gave her my last name. She was my everything. I was hoping that maybe she just needed time to figure out how to tell me.

I just hope she knows that I'm killing her brother, soon she would feel the same hurt, and betrayal I feel right now.

Lauren:

Pulling up to my house was painful, I was nervous and my stomach was in knots. I watched the love of my life hurt for months and now I knew the answer but how could I tell him? I knew there would be no peaceful solution Jayson would kill him!

How could I hand deliver my brother's fate?

He was my blood. He was everything to me. I was so mad at him but I had to protect him somehow. I loved Jayson with my entire heart, he was the best thing that ever happened to me but I owed Kyree all the LOYALTY in the world.

THE END…………..

About the Author

Shateria A. Franklin is a Native of Erie, Pennsylvania born in Pittsburgh Pennsylvania. She is the mother of two boys that she loves dearly David & Major. She is a graduate of Gannon University with a Bachelors of Arts in Criminal Justice and Pre- Law. She is also completing her Master's Degree in Criminology at Gannon University. She began writing Love & Loyalty in early 2011 and put it off for quiet sometime as life began to happen. My best advice is to never ever give up on your dreams and goals no matter what happens in your life. If you can believe it then you can do it with faith in God and the work you put in you will accomplish your goal.

This book is for the hardworking beautiful woman that may have been through somethings but they wake up daily, put their best foot forward, and get it done. I see you ladies and I appreciate and respect your hustle. Keep going do not give up! Continue to prepare for your season because when it comes no one will be able to STOP you! Whatever God has prepared for you is for you and you ONLY!

Thank you for reading and be on the lookout for Part 2 coming soon!

Follow her on social media:

Instagram: @msshateria

Snap Chat: Iamshateria

With Love, Shateria A. Franklin.

This book is dedicated to my children David Jr and Major,

my mother Terri and my late father Johnnie C. Thank you

for always loving and supporting me through everything.

A special thank you to you! Yes, you know who you are

thank you for your constant motivation. THIS ONE IS FOR

YOU Baby!!!!!!

A special thanks to my life long best friend/ sister Genovia

for contributing to the cover for this project you have seen

me through this entire process and you provide both love and

loyalty without a price. Love you best friend!!!